Elizabeth's Choice

Linda Lyle

Heartsong Presents

To God who gave me just a hint of His creativity
and
To my parents who believed in me.

A note from the author:
I love to hear from my readers! You may correspond with me by writing:
            Linda Lyle
            Author Relations
            PO Box 719
            Uhrichsville, OH 44683

ISBN 1-57748-333-2

ELIZABETH'S CHOICE

Cover illustration by Brian Bowman.

PRINTED IN THE U.S.A.

one

Elizabeth pushed back a stray hair as she worked on the computer. Engrossed in her research, she didn't hear Alex McClintock come up behind her, and she jumped at the sound of his voice.

"Morning, Elizabeth."

"Good morning, Mr. McClintock." She tried to look businesslike, but her hands trembled on the keyboard. She kept her eyes glued to the screen.

"Just call me Alex."

"Yes, sir. What can I do for you?"

"Stop calling me sir."

"Oh. . .I'm sorry. . .Alex."

"That's better. I need some research done for the Brennan case." He handed her the file, complete with a list of detailed instructions.

"Yes, sir. I mean, Alex."

"Leave it on my desk when you're through." He put the file on top of the stack she was working on, hesitating before giving it a final tap. Elizabeth looked up.

"Anything else?" she asked.

"No. That's it. I'll let you get back to work." In two quick strides he was out of her office.

Elizabeth watched the tall figure move down the hall. Realizing she was staring, she turned back to her work, her face flushed. What was she thinking? There was no way Alex McClintock was going to give her a moment's notice. She might as well get it out of her head right now. She pushed away from the desk with a groan. He wasn't her type anyway. Why did she care what he thought? He was a playboy, a flirt. He wasn't serious about settling down. Pushing the files away in frustration, she put her elbows on the desk and rested her chin in her hands.

More than anything, she wanted to get out of this rat race. What if she married Alex? She could picture the two of them living in a Victorian house with two children and a dog. Once, she had mentioned her ideal to a co-worker, only to be scolded for being so old-fashioned. Old-fashioned or not, one day she wanted to quit work and raise a family.

The shrill ring of the telephone brought her out of her reverie. With a sigh, she picked up the phone and went back to work. A couple of hours later, she gathered the last of the information for the Brennan file and headed for Alex's office, her heart rate increasing as she neared his office. Scolding herself, she took a deep breath and knocked on the open door.

"I have the Brennan file ready."

"Great." He flipped through the folder and nodded in approval. "Thanks for getting it done so quickly. I have a dinner meeting with Mr. Brennan tonight." She turned to leave, but he motioned for her to wait. "What are you doing for lunch?"

"Lunch?"

"Yes, you know, that thing people do around noon?"

"I know what lunch means, but. . ."

"Good, then I'll pick you up in an hour." Without another word he returned to his work. Elizabeth walked out of the office and turned the wrong way in the hallway. She caught herself just before she entered the men's room and with red cheeks made her way back to her office. Sinking into her chair, she wondered if she had heard right. Had Alex really asked her out to lunch?

Looking at her reflection in the computer screen, she wondered what would possess him to do such a thing. He had it all: charm, good looks, money. She was known as the poor ice maiden who couldn't get a date. She had never been one for casual dating, but her conservative upbringing tended to send guys running in the opposite direction. Once, she had even overheard the guys in the office betting on who could thaw the "ice princess." She had spent her break crying in the ladies' room. From then on she had vowed to be very cautious about whom she dated. For the life of her, she couldn't figure out why she had agreed to go out with Alex. *Yes you do,* a little voice whispered. Ever since she had begun working at the offices of McClintock & McClintock, she had found herself fascinated by the senior partner and eldest son of Matthew McClintock. Every time she got around him, her throat constricted and her mind refused to work. With his dark good looks, he could have been a model, but with the added assets of intelligence and charm, he made a formidable lawyer. He was the kind of man women fantasized about, Elizabeth included. She would have to watch her step this time, because she knew it wouldn't take much to fall prey to his charms. She sighed and tried to shake off the image of her and Alex dancing in the moonlight and got her mind back on the job at hand.

At five minutes before noon, Alex breezed into her office. "Ready to go." It was more a statement than a question.

"Just let me save this information on a file."

"No rush." He smiled that easy smile, and she had doubts about what she was doing. He had a reputation with the ladies. She was way out of her league, but curiosity got the better of her.

"I'll get my jacket."

"Here, let me do that." As he helped her into her jacket, his hand rested on her shoulder for a second longer than necessary, and when they moved toward the door, Elizabeth released a breath. The man never failed to make her nervous.

He escorted her out of the building and into his Mercedes, passing several obviously surprised co-workers. As they passed Inner Harbor, she realized they were headed for Little Italy. Elizabeth watched the flurry of activity as boats of all descriptions dotted the waterway. It was her favorite place to visit. A smile played at the corners of her mouth as she remembered walks along the harbor with her roommates and eating crabcakes at the harborside cafes.

"What are you thinking about?"

"Oh, I was just thinking how much I love living here in Baltimore." There was little else said on the ride to the restaurant. Maybe he was as nervous as she was, but somehow she doubted that Alex was ever nervous. A quick glance at his profile confirmed her suspicions. He was as cool as ever.

They arrived and were ushered immediately to the best table in the house. Elizabeth noticed that the waiters treated him with a familiar deference. This obviously wasn't his first time here. She picked up the linen napkin and placed it in her lap, toying with the ends.

"What would you like?" The waiter stood patiently while she studied the menu—all the Italian names were confusing. She glanced down at her blouse in dismay. She had a tendency to spill when she was nervous, and today she was wearing a white silk blouse that was sure to stain. Unable to make a clear decision she suddenly remembered a piece of advice her mother had given when she had first started dating: when in doubt, let the man order. So, she gave him a lopsided smile and said, "I'm not sure. What do you suggest?"

After Alex ordered for both of them, the waiter nodded and disappeared. That was the mark of a good restaurant, silent service. She was surprised to find that Alex actually seemed interested in her. He asked her questions about her views on the recent election. He looked directly into her eyes and seemed to hang on her every word, despite the fact that she knew little about the election. His obvious interest made her nervous. She focused on the spot directly above his tie, but not quite into his eyes. He reached out and lifted her chin.

"I can't see those beautiful brown eyes when you keep looking at my tie."

"I'm. . .sorry," she stuttered. When the food came, she had a moment of panic. What if she spilled the sauce on her new white blouse?

"I hope you like manicotti. It's safer than spaghetti," he sid as if reading her mind and pointing to his crisp white shirt. "I can't go to a meeting with tomato sauce on my shirt. I keep an extra white shirt and tie in my car for emergencies."

He smiled and she relaxed. He was good company. They talked about books, music, the theatre, and found they had several things in common. Before she knew it, she had agreed to go to a dinner party with him on Saturday night. When they returned to the office, Elizabeth had a sparkle in her eye and no desire to work. She found her mind replaying lunch over and over again. She looked forward to Saturday night like Cinderella anticipating the ball. The lull soon passed and she found little time for daydreaming.

The week flew by in a flurry of business meetings, last-minute research, and a ton of paperwork. It was Saturday morning before Elizabeth even had time to look for something to wear to the dinner party. She chided herself over and over for not thinking about it earlier in the week. But, then again, she really hadn't had time to think about it. If she had, she probably would have canceled the date. A search through her wardrobe found it sadly inadequate for the occasion. She tried on a blue satin dress that looked like it belonged on a bridesmaid. Then she pulled out a suit dress with a long skirt, but it looked too professional.

She finally decided on a simple, black velvet dress which covered her from neck to toe with a slit up the front to allow for walking. She fussed with her straight hair, but when the doorbell rang twenty minutes later her hair looked the same.

She looked through the peephole. Even from this view, Alex was breathtaking in a black tuxedo. She opened the door, and he looked even better from this distance. She realized she must have been staring when he said, "Are you going to let me in or were you expecting someone else?"

"Oh! I'm sorry. Come in." She moved back to let him in and mentally kicked herself for being so obvious. She had wanted to appear sophisticated, and now she felt awkward, like a teenager on her first date. "I'll just get my coat and I'll be ready." She tried to walk gracefully across the room, but stumbled on the edge of the rug. She was sure he had to have seen her, but he appeared completely absorbed by the pictures on the wall.

"No rush. We'll be fashionably late." He smiled and she tried to steady her lips into a returning one. She may live to regret this night.

They arrived as predicted, fashionably late. It seemed everyone arrived ten minutes after the time stated on the invitation. A butler took their invitation and coats, and then they were ushered into the largest room Elizabeth had ever seen in a home. Alex barely had time to make any introductions before dinner was called. She found herself between Alex and a balding man in his forties.

Elizabeth looked around as the appetizer was served. "It's the fork on the end dear," her dinner partner whispered, but Elizabeth didn't miss the patronizing smirk.

"Thank you."

"Anytime."

Elizabeth toyed with her napkin and glanced at the grandfather clock. Only seven. She'd never make it. But make it she did through three courses of boring conversation served with a side of sarcasm. She managed not to catapult the crab legs across the room as she cracked them open or spill butter sauce on her dress. And just when she brought the last bite of chocolate mousse to her mouth, the man next to her jostled her and sent the morsel flying into a crystal vase filled with Birds of Paradise. She couldn't have hit it if she had tried. Glancing around, she breathed a sigh of relief. Everyone was too absorbed in conversation to notice. It was at that moment that their host chose to make an announcement.

"Let's have coffee and brandy in the music room." She had never actually believed that people had a room just for music.

"Brandy, Miss?"

"No, thank you." She didn't drink, another reason to dislike these parties.

"A soda or mineral water, perhaps." Elizabeth considered ginger ale, but she didn't want people to think she was drinking. She felt conspicuous with her hands empty, but she refused the offer and looked around for Alex. She wouldn't feel so much like an intruder if she were with him. She spotted him across the room, talking with a judge and a senator.

"I say, Senator, what do you think of the election? Think it will change anything in the White House?"

"Interesting question, but what intrigues me is. . ."

Elizabeth's attention moved to the two men standing beside her, arguing over who would make the final four. The group of women behind her in their designer originals were discussing the merits of a certain caterer. She stood in the sea of colors and sounds looking for somewhere to melt into the background. Finally, she noticed French doors on her right and slipped into the relative quiet of the garden.

Alex found her there an hour later. "So this is where you disappeared to. I was beginning to think someone had kidnapped you."

"At this point, I'd pay someone to kidnap me."

"It's not that bad now, is it?" He smiled that smile.

"I guess not."

"You guess not. Come on. It's business, a necessary evil. I'd much rather be alone with you." He moved closer and took her hand.

"Then let's go. All this buzzing is giving me a headache."

"What buzzing?"

"All this noise. Everybody talking and no one saying anything. It sounds like static on the radio when you're getting two stations at one time." Her voice faded away as she realized how foolish she sounded.

He laughed sending shivers up her spine. "Are you cold?"

"A little," she said.

"Come on. I'll take you home."

He said very little on the way home, but he kept possession of her hand even after they were in the car, letting go only long enough to get in and get the car moving. When they pulled up in front of her small townhouse, she made a move to get out, but he pulled her back.

"It's early. Let's go in and talk for a little while."

She hesitated. "I. . .I. . ." Something in the back of her mind said no, but he left little room for argument. He came around and opened the car door and then asked for her keys to unlock the apartment door. She barely had time to think of a proper response before he was already in the apartment.

"Let's listen to some quiet music and sit and talk."

"Help yourself." She motioned toward a boom box next to the TV and a portable cassette case holder and a small selection of CDs. He chose some quiet blues and then drew her onto the couch. He smiled and put his arm around her, her head on his shoulder.

"That's better." He ran his fingers through her hair and she shivered again. "Are you cold?" Before she could answer, he wrapped his arms around her, and she could feel the heat from his body through her dress. She felt uncomfortable and flushed, but another part of her was curious. She had never done this sort of thing before, mainly because she never went out very much.

"Your hair is so soft, I could get lost in it." He buried his face in the dark tresses and then placed a soft kiss on her neck. She could smell the scent of alcohol on his breath. Then suddenly, he was kissing her lips and her lips parted. She pulled away. It was happening all over again.

"What's the matter?"

"I'm just not ready for this."

"Come on, sweetheart. Just relax."

"I just think we're moving a little fast. I really don't know you that well."

"Well, let's get to know each other." He pulled her back into his arms and his hands began to move. She grabbed his hands and pushed him away.

"I said no. Now stop."

"What's wrong with you. We were just having a little fun."

"I wasn't."

"It didn't seem that way to me. You seemed to be enjoying yourself."

She blushed, but stood her ground. "Look. I'm not interested. Maybe you should find someone more your type."

"Maybe I should."

He grabbed his coat on his way out the door. When she heard his car start up and speed away, she released a breath. Bolting the door, she began to get ready for bed, but his words haunted her. The Bible on her nightstand seemed to accuse her, and instant replays of her behavior brought a flush of shame to her cheeks. She tried to put it out of her mind, but memories of the way he had held her hand and the feel of his arms around her filled her thoughts. A wave of longing for someone to hold her brought wracking sobs from within. The loneliness she had felt since her parents' deaths wrapped its cold arms around her, and she shivered in the dark.

When would it be her turn? She had watched all her friends date and marry and move away. Why was it that she was left alone? Just when she thought her prince had come along, he had turned into a frog. Even the absurd image of Alex as a frog couldn't dispel the shadows. In the dark, she raised her pleas to heaven, but there was silence. She snuggled deeper into the covers and turned to her imagination for comfort. For in her dreams, Alex returned and begged for her forgiveness, saying he was so overcome by his love for her that he was unable to control himself. But the cold light of morning broke the spell and Elizabeth knew that Alex was just like the others.

two

Alex's anger was boiling underneath the surface. He appeared the essence of calm—he always managed to keep his temper buried. His motto was "Don't get mad, get even," and he always did. He walked to his car and closed the door with care. He drove the usual speed home, but part of him wanted to speed or curse the other drivers, do something to release his frustration. But instead he continued to drive and plan. He would make her pay somehow. She wanted to play ice maiden, but he would thaw her out. He always got what he wanted, and right now he wanted her, at least for a little while. He hadn't had a good challenge in a long time. With the decision made, he relaxed and began to enjoy the drive.

His mind wandered back to Monday morning. He had been in Jacobson's office when Elizabeth brought in some files. Her smile had faltered when she sensed his presence. Her reputation as an ice princess intrigued him, especially since his very presence seemed to intimidate her. He liked that. At lunch, she had let him take care of everything and had refused to even look him in the eye. He had figured that it would not be too hard to bring her around to his way of thinking, but he hadn't counted on her strong sense of morality. He had thought it was a cover for her fear of men. Well, now he would just have to change his plan of attack.

At home, he made himself a martini. He made it a point to make his own drinks at night. He didn't like the servants keeping tabs on his drinking habits. His desk was in perfect order as always and he sighed in satisfaction. The night had not gone as planned, but all was not lost. He smiled over the rim of his glass at the prospect of victory. He savored the martini and then worked until the wee hours of the morning.

Sunday, he didn't wake until noon. The blinds were drawn

so that the room remained dark despite the rays of sunshine that threatened to burst through. Alex was dimly aware of the servants moving quietly about their work. He ran a tight ship with no room for argument. One act of disobedience resulted in termination. His orders were carried out to the letter without question, as it should be. He stretched in bed and contemplated the day. A ring of the bedside bell brought a manservant with his breakfast and morning paper.

The telephone rang and he frowned. No one called him at home on Sunday. He picked up the receiver to the sound of his brother's voice. Golden Boy wanted to know why he hadn't come for lunch. Alex made a quick excuse and hung up the phone. It never failed to amaze him how blind his brother was. Scott just couldn't fathom why he wouldn't want to spend every Sunday possible at home. He had to work all week with their father. Wasn't that enough?

His entire life had been run by their tyrannical father. There were rules for everything, especially regarding conduct. Every Sunday was filled with lessons about character both in Sunday school and at home. Now Alex made the rules.

He remembered how he had worked so hard to please his father. But nothing he did was ever good enough. When he was ten, he had won the 50-yard dash at school, but instead of saying, "Good job, son," his father had said, "We'll work on cutting your time on Saturday." When he was twelve, he had competed in another track event. Trying to impress his father with a victory, he had tripped another runner in order to win. The judges hadn't seen, but his father had railed on him about fair play and honesty. He had forced Alex to return the medal and confess. The humiliation still burned today.

Then Scott had come along—he could do nothing wrong. There was never a moment when he wasn't in the spotlight. He had been a straight-A student, the model citizen, and an outstanding athlete. Even when Golden Boy did something wrong, the punishments were never as severe as Alex had received. When Scott had taken the car without permission and hit the mailbox, he only received a slight reprimand and had to wait an extra month to get his license. When Alex had taken the car without his father's knowledge and gone to a party at a friend's house, he had been grounded for a month and had to endure one of his father's sermons on the kinds of friends he should have.

He shook his head to clear away the memories. That was then, and this was now. He was in control of his own life now, thawing out Elizabeth Jordan.

Obviously, she had been raised in the same kind of atmosphere as he had. He knew how to play that game. He had enough examples to follow in how to be holy on Sunday and devilish on Saturday night. The church he grew up in had plenty of Sunday-only Christians. Deacon Hemsley could be seen in the hottest nightspots in town with a pretty girl on his arm on any Friday night, but every Sunday he was with his wife and children nodding in agreement to the preacher's sermons on the evils of hypocrisy and adultery. All he had to do was convince Elizabeth that he was a Christian who had made a wrong turn on the road and needed a little push in the right direction. As soon as he had gained her trust, it wouldn't take long to reel her in. Alex smiled to himself as the plans formed in his mind.

He placed a call to the most expensive florist in town and ordered their most impressive roses. Some flowers and a little charm went a long way. He hung up and stretched in bed. Yes, that would do nicely.

Monday morning he arrived early with the roses. He signed the card and left it with the flowers on Elizabeth's desk. He smiled the smile that had led many astray as he walked back to his office. It wouldn't be long now.

At ten o'clock, Janice announced Scott's arrival. That's all he needed to start off his Monday. He told her to show him in and then plastered a smile on his face. By the time the door opened, Alex even looked pleased to see his baby brother.

"Morning, Golden Boy," Alex greeted, coming around the desk to slap Scott on the back.

"Hi, Alex." Alex could tell by the slight frown that the

nickname still annoyed his little brother.

"What can I do for you?"

"Just thought I'd drop in since I was in the building."

"I thought the reason you didn't join the firm was that you hated being stuck in an office. What could possibly bring you in voluntarily?" The sarcasm in his voice obviously grated, but Scott remained calm, a fact which never ceased to irritate Alex.

Ignoring Alex's comment, Scott said, "I need some help with some legal paperwork. Dad's arranging a meeting with one of your researchers."

"I'm sure he is."

"Mom missed you yesterday," Scott said, shifting his weight.

"Mmm." Alex leaned over the paperwork on his desk, but Scott didn't take the hint.

"She made your favorite. Chocolate Mousse."

"Oh. That's nice."

"Look at me when I'm talking to you."

Alex looked up with an air of resignation. "Do we have to go through this again?"

"Yeah. We do. After all they've done for you, you can't even take a few hours out of your busy schedule to eat lunch with them." Scott's arms were folded over his chest in an obvious effort to hold his temper. Alex sighed and then leaned forward in his chair.

"I don't see the need to spend my day off driving way out there, just to eat lunch. I see Dad every day in the office."

"What about Mom?" Alex could see the frustration building in Scott's every movement.

"Despite what you think, I do visit her occasionally."

"You mean holidays and birthdays. That just doesn't cut it." Scott's mouth tightened into a thin line.

"That's my decision, not yours, Golden Boy." Alex stood up and walked around the desk. "Now, if you don't mind, I have work to do." Alex held the door open as Scott stalked from the room. "See you later, Golden Boy." As the door closed, the smile faded from his lips.

three

Monday morning, Elizabeth found a dozen roses on her desk with a card that read, "I'm sorry. Please forgive me, signed Alex." She still felt ashamed and wasn't exactly sure why. Girls her age, nice girls, did as much as she did Saturday night and no one thought any less of them. Yet she couldn't shake the feeling. Maybe because his words had a ring of truth in them. She had encouraged him in the beginning. She touched the roses and felt the silky petals. No one had ever given her flowers. She sighed and tried to put the whole thing out of her mind and immersed herself in the Brennan case.

At lunch, she was called into Mr. McClintock Senior's office. He was a tall and distinguished looking man. He had lost the healthy build of his son and retained the height, making him appear feeble. But the image was quickly dispelled when he moved around in a courtroom. He was an imposing figure in his element.

"Miss Jordan. I want you to research an estate settlement. My son Scott needs the information for a job he's doing for me. He'll be here shortly. Why don't you have a seat until he gets here. If you'll excuse me, I'll make some calls."

Elizabeth took a seat at the conference table he had pointed out and got out a legal pad and pen. While she waited, she tried to remember what she had heard about Scott McClintock. He had opted out of the family business, instead starting his own construction firm. The girls in the office said he was cute but difficult to get to know. She would find out soon enough.

The door opened and a younger, more rugged Alex walked into the room, but the similarities stopped there. There was no smooth smile or polished greeting.

"This is Miss Jordan who will be doing your research. Miss

Jordan, this is my son Scott McClintock. I'll let you two get to work." Mr. McClintock returned to the stack of papers on his desk, and Scott held out his hand.

"Nice to meet you."

"Nice to meet you, Mr. McClintock."

"Call me Scott. He's Mr. McClintock." He gestured toward his father. "What's your name?"

"Elizabeth."

"Well, Elizabeth, if you can't tell, I didn't follow in the family business. I run a construction firm that renovates abandoned warehouses into apartments and condominiums. So, I don't know a lot about some of this legal mumbo jumbo. That's what I need you for."

"It's nice to be needed."

"I like the way you think. Where are you from?"

"Alabama."

"You're a long way from home!"

"Well, I don't have any family there anymore, and this is my home now."

"I'm sorry to hear that. Would I be nosy if I asked about your family?"

"Not when you ask so nicely. My parents died my freshman year in college, and I'm an only child. So, I just stayed here after graduation."

"Where did you go to school?"

"University of Maryland, where else?"

He smiled and chuckled. "Of course. When did you start work here?"

"I got an intern job here my Sophomore year and stayed on as an aide until I finished my degree." She pointed her pen at him. "What about you?"

"I guess that's only fair. I graduated from the University of Maryland, too, but not the law school. I got a degree in business."

"How did you get into construction work?"

He laughed and leaned back in his chair. "When I was in high school, I volunteered with my church to work with

Habitat for Humanity. I liked it so much that I spent my summers working for a local contractor. He taught me the ropes. So here I am."

Mr. McClintock eyed them from his desk, and their smiles quickly vanished into stern businesslike expressions.

"Okay. Let's get to work."

He was easy to work with, and she forgot all about Alex as they researched the estate of a Mr. Charles Bowden. He had owned an old warehouse on the harbor which he was in the process of selling to McClintock Construction. He needed some help with the deeds and getting a contract ready. Unlike Alex, he didn't try to run the conversation or try to use words meant to impress people. She liked that. She liked him.

"Well, I guess that's it. Let me know when you get the papers ready. I'll be at this number during the day, and this is my home number. I'm usually home every night, except Wednesday. That's Bible study."

"Bible study? Where?"

"At my church in Cedar Heights. You're welcome to come."

"I've been looking for a church. What denomination is it?"

"Nondenominational."

"Great. Where is it?"

He took out a business card and drew a rough map on the back, making a note of the times for services.

"Thanks."

"You're welcome any time." He smiled, and she sensed he meant what he said. "Bye."

"Bye." She gathered her papers and returned to her desk. She tapped the card on her desk and then put it in her daytimer. How could two brothers look so much alike and be so different. Scott obviously preferred the great outdoors to an office. Elizabeth just couldn't picture Alex with any kind of tool in his hands. He might break a nail. She laughed at the mental image of Alex trying to figure out how to use a hammer. Brushing aside all thoughts of Alex, Elizabeth focused on Scott. She was still thinking about him as she cleaned up her desk for the night, a smile played around her lips.

"Hello, Elizabeth." Her smile faded at the sound of his voice.

"Alex."

"Is that all you have to say?"

"It's the best I can do at the moment." She straightened the files on her desk, her eyes on the stack.

"Would you please look at me." He reached out and pulled her chin up until she was forced to look into his eyes. "That's better."

"What do you want?"

"I want to make up. Forgive and forget. I said I was sorry. What else do you want?"

"I just want to forget it." She pulled away from him and reached for her purse and coat.

"Here, let me help you with that." He took the coat from her hand and held it out. She sighed and slipped into the coat. His hands didn't linger this time. Maybe he had learned his lesson. Maybe not.

"Let's just forget the whole thing. You go your way, and I'll go mine, and we won't think or talk about it anymore. Okay?"

"But I don't want to go my way and you go yours. Give me another chance."

"Look, we're just too different. We don't have enough in common."

"How do you know? You said yourself that you didn't know me very well. Give yourself a chance to get to know me. Give me a chance."

She sighed again. He was so pushy. Why couldn't he just drop it? She pushed her hair away from her face. "I'm really not interested. Now, if you'll excuse me, I'm going home."

"Alone?"

"Of course, alone." Her temper flared. She was getting tired of this.

"If you keep running away from every relationship, you're going to end up that way. Permanently." He turned and left, giving her no time to respond.

How dare he? Why did men insist on butting in where they weren't wanted? Suddenly tired, she gathered up her purse and gloves and headed for home.

On the drive home, she kept replaying the conversation in her mind. The more she thought about it, the angrier she got. At the house, she dropped all her things on the table at the front door. She flipped through the mail, but there was nothing but bills. She opened every cabinet in the kitchen, but nothing looked good. She finally grabbed a frozen dinner and sat down in front of the TV. She took turns eating and channel surfing. Forty channels and nothing worth watching. She turned off the TV and went to her room with a book, but she couldn't concentrate. A little voice kept saying, "What if he's right?" She didn't want to end up alone. Was she unconsciously keeping men at a distance? She went to bed early, spending the night tossing and turning.

She groaned at the sound of the alarm. Untangling her arms from the bedclothes, she hit the off button and rolled over. Thoughts of Alex made her close her eyes and go back to sleep. Twenty minutes later she woke up and jerked the covers off. Instead of her normal leisurely cup of coffee, watching the birds at the birdfeeder, she rushed through her shower and changed clothes three times. Nothing seemed to fit anymore. A quick look at the scale told her why. She left for work with a very bad attitude.

four

Elizabeth spent Tuesday avoiding Alex, though he didn't try to corner her again. She let out a deep breath as she headed for home.

Wednesday she went to work with a lighter step. As she was going through the day's mail, the phone rang.

"Research."

"Hi, Elizabeth. This is Hope."

"How are you? It's so good to hear from you. I thought you guys had fallen off the earth."

"We're doing fine. I'm sorry we haven't gotten with you sooner. As a matter of fact, that's why I called. We're having a dinner party, well actually a very informal dinner. Just you and Stacey and Bart. We haven't seen each other in so long that I thought this would be a good time to get together."

"I'd love that. When?"

"Well, I know it's short notice, but can you come tonight?"

"Sure. I don't have any plans. It'll be great not to have to cook."

"Right. You can relax until time to wash the dishes."

"Yeah. Right. It'll be like old times when the three of us lived together. You'll mess up the kitchen, and I'll clean it up." They both laughed.

"Then we'll see you tonight."

"Okay. Hey, what time?"

"Just come directly from work. Then we can catch up until everybody gets here."

"Okay. See you then."

"Bye." Elizabeth hung up the phone and smiled. It was the first good news she'd had in a while. It would be nice to see her old roommates.

They had all met in law school. Stacey was a would-be

lawyer with dreams of beating the lions of injustice single-handedly, and Hope was in college to make her parents happy. They had met in Ethics and decided to move into a small house together and split the rent. Hope had been miserable until Jeff, an aspiring litigation lawyer, had arrived on the scene. It didn't take Hope long to realize what she really wanted out of life. Being a lawyer had been her mother's dream. All Hope wanted was to have a family and settle down, which was tantamount to mutiny in a feminist society. Stacey had wanted nothing to do with men, but she was no match for Bart. He wore her down until she begged for mercy. The weddings were back to back the June after graduation. She could remember their good times together as if it was yesterday, but it was becoming a speck on the horizon. Elizabeth shook off the shadow of gloom that threatened to choke out her joy.

She turned to her work with a vengeance, hoping to speed up the clock. The day drug by at a snail's pace, compounded by the computer shutting down for an hour which slowed the pace even more. Still, she was surprised when she glanced at her watch and found it was time to leave for Hope's house in the suburbs. As she neared the house, a sign caught her eye. "Cedar Heights Community Church." Scott McClintock's face came to her mind, and she looked around with more interest. She blushed when she realized that she was looking for any sign of him and was glad no one was around to see her. Elizabeth zipped through the last three intersections. Whipping into their driveway, she squeaked to a halt and bounded out, slamming the door and fairly skipping up the drive. As she raised her hand to knock, the door burst open. Hope greeted her with a big hug and a squeal of delight. "It's so great to see you. Come on in." Hope pulled her in, closed the door, and took her coat almost at the same time, leaving Elizabeth breathless.

"Where's Jeff?"

"He's in the kitchen pretending he's a master chef."

"Did I just hear my name being maligned?" Jeff stood in

the doorway, his broad shoulders leaving little space, his blue eyes dancing. He came over and gave Elizabeth a bear hug.

"Hey, honey." Elizabeth returned.

"Watch who you're calling honey," Hope scolded, but her eyes smiled.

"Well, I feel like he's our fourth roommate. He did everything but sleep at our apartment. Couldn't get rid of the guy." Elizabeth playfully punched Jeff in the arm.

Jeff put his arm around her shoulders. "That's right, and I reserve the right to call her pumpkin." He rumpled Elizabeth's hair.

"Watch it or I'll pumpkin you. When will Stacey and Bart be here?" Elizabeth asked.

"They said about six thirty, but knowing those two it will probably be seven. Jeff, why don't you show her our vacation pictures of Hawaii while I check on dinner."

"Okay, darling."

"That's much better." Hope patted him on the head and returned to the kitchen. Elizabeth flipped through pictures of Jeff and Hope snorkeling, swimming, sunbathing, and hiking. They were always together, smiling and happy. A knot formed in her throat, and she tried to swallow down the wave of self-pity that threatened to choke her. She was on the verge of a pity party when the doorbell rang. Thankful for the distraction, she closed the album with a snap.

"I'll get it," Jeff yelled. "Look who's on time for a change. They're only ten minutes late instead of thirty."

"Very funny, Jeff. It was all his fault?" Stacey wagged her finger at Bart.

"My fault?" Bart put his hands on his hips. "What do you mean, my fault. You're the one who changed clothes twice and then had to redo your lipstick."

"Yeah, but I would have been ready on time if you hadn't kept asking me where is this and where is that. I spent more time getting you ready than me."

"Likely story," Jeff rang in.

"Hush now, before you get a fight started," Hope said, drying her hand on a towel.

"Too late," Jeff responded. They all laughed and hugs were swapped all around. There was a general bustle as coats were taken and people settled into chairs. Elizabeth looked around. It was nice to be back with the old gang. It wasn't very often that she got to relax and be herself. Everyone she had hung around with in law school was married now and busy with their new lives.

"Hey, when's dinner?" Jeff said, patting his stomach.

"Dinner will be served as soon as you set the table," Hope replied.

"A man's work is never done," Jeff groaned as he started to get out of his recliner.

"Never mind, I'll do it," Elizabeth said as she headed toward the kitchen.

"Okay," Jeff said, relaxing quickly into his recliner.

Elizabeth found Hope already in the kitchen getting out the plates and silverware. Hope smiled when she saw Elizabeth. "So Jeff suckered you into doing his job?" She knew Jeff all too well. Elizabeth reached for the napkins and started setting the places.

"So, anything new?" Hope asked.

"You mean, have I met anyone new?" Hope had the grace to look embarrassed. "It's okay and the answer is yes and no."

"What do you mean yes and no? Give it up, girl. I want details." Hope's eyes danced with anticipation.

"Don't get so excited. It's nothing. I'll probably never see him again."

"See who again?" Stacey asked from the doorway.

Elizabeth groaned. "Nothing. It's nothing. Really."

"Did you or did you not go out on a date with a man?" Stacey was in her courtroom stance questioning the witness.

"Yes, but we only went out once, well twice actually. But it didn't mean anything."

"The witness is contradicting herself. She must be lying.

Now, out with the truth before we hold you in contempt of court." Stacey's eyes had taken on the look of a hunter closing in on its prey.

"All right already. I'll confess." Elizabeth threw up her hands in mock defeat. "I'll tell everything I know."

"That's more like it." Stacey smiled in satisfaction. "I knew I could make her talk. Bart says it's one of my many talents."

"Come on, girl. Tell all." Hope grabbed her arms and pulled her over to the breakfast nook and Stacey closed the kitchen door.

"What about dinner? The boys will be getting hungry," Elizabeth protested.

"They'll live. Besides, I'm hungry for information, and Bart knows better than to get in my way when I'm after the truth," Stacey responded.

"Okay." Elizabeth sighed and then told them about lunch with Alex and the dinner party, but she left out the incident in her apartment. Stacey looked satisfied, but Hope gave her that "I know you're not telling me everything" look.

"He sounds great. He's tall, dark, handsome, and rich. What more could you ask for?" Stacey asked.

"I don't know. I just feel out of place when I'm around his friends. I'm not used to all that."

"Well, you'll get used to it. I think it sounds fabulous. You get to meet all those important people and eat in expensive restaurants. I bet he would be the kind to buy expensive jewelry." Stacey was excited.

"Is that all you think about?" Hope chided. "I guess so. That's why you married Bart." They all burst into laughter.

"Hey, what's all this? Where's our dinner?" Bart demanded from the doorway. "He-man heap big hungry." He beat his chest and let out a Tarzan yell. The girls' laughter didn't stop until dinner was served and they paused for prayer.

Dinner was Hope's specialty, lasagna with a Caesar's salad on the side and hot garlic rolls. They ate and joked between mouth fulls. The subject of Alex was dropped until after

Stacey and Bart excused themselves later that night.

"Well, we hate to eat and run, but we need the exercise," Stacey said as she patted Bart's slightly protruding stomach. "Seriously, I have a meeting in New York Thursday night and I still have to pack."

"I wish you could stay longer," Hope replied.

"Me too. We need to do this again, soon. I miss you guys." Stacey hugged Elizabeth and Hope.

"Hey, what about me?" Jeff put on his fake hurt look. Stacey laughed and gave him a hug. "That's better." After several more good-byes, Hope shut the door and Jeff took his cue.

"I'll be upstairs in my office if you need me. I've got some figures to go over. See you again soon, Elizabeth." With a hug and a wave, he bounded up the stairs. It was time for "a talk."

"Why don't we go in the living room and talk?"

"What about the dishes?" Elizabeth was stalling and Hope knew it.

"They can wait. Now what's all this about Alex?" she asked as she sunk into the sofa. Elizabeth joined her.

"What do you mean? I told you and Stacey all about it in the kitchen."

"No you didn't. You left something out. I can tell. I know you better than anyone." This was true. Hope had been her only close friend since she came to Baltimore. Elizabeth let out a long breath.

"I don't know. It's just that I'm not sure he's the kind of guy that I want to date." She told Hope about that night. "You see I feel so. . .I don't know. . .ashamed since that night."

"Why? You didn't do anything wrong."

"That's what I keep trying to tell myself, but I can't get away from the feeling that I shouldn't have gone out with him in the first place."

"Well if that's the way you feel, then don't see him anymore."

"Easier said than done. He sent me flowers and asked me

out again. He apologized for the other night. But when I refused to go out with him again, he said that I was going to end up lonely if I didn't quit running from men. Do you think I'm running away from men?" Elizabeth asked, her face a study in turmoil.

"I don't think so, honey, but you're going to have to decide that for yourself. Pray about it. Ask God for guidance. That's the best advice I can give you." Hope patted her hand and gave her a sympathetic smile. "Now let's not talk about him anymore."

True to her word, Hope didn't mention Alex again. They spent the next hour catching up on the little things going on in their lives. An hour and a half later, Elizabeth found herself passing Cedar Heights Community Church. She automatically thought of Scott McClintock, and she wondered where his house was located. She glanced at the church in her rearview mirror, and she remembered Hope's advice.

"Lord, I don't know what to do. Help me." She whispered the prayer and a tear escaped and fell on her cheek. She was reminded of the Psalm, "Delight thyself also in the LORD; and he shall give thee the desires of thine heart." It echoed in her mind the rest of the drive home.

five

Icy fingers touched her skin as she left the warmth of the townhouse. Elizabeth pulled the coat tighter around her throat, but the cold seemed to slip through imaginary cracks in the material. Before she made it to her car, rain began to fall. As she slammed the car door against the rain, she looked out in disgust. With the temperatures this cold, it was a wonder it wasn't snowing. Anything would be better than this dismal rain, which left the streets and sidewalks muddy and her clothes damp. By the time she got to work, Elizabeth's mood matched the weather.

As the day went by, the rain fell in sheets, leaving the city in a foggy shroud. Work poured in, leaving Elizabeth in a white cloak of paper. Everyone had a problem, and they all thought she had the answer. Just when she was getting ready to do some serious work, the computer system slowed until she felt like she was caught in a traffic jam. The weather even seemed to affect the computer system.

By lunch, Elizabeth's mood had deteriorated to a really bad attitude. If Alex had only known, he would have steered clear of her office. Instead, at ten minutes before twelve, he came in all smiles and charm. His cheery hello was like adding dry ice to water.

"What do you want?" was her less-than-polite response.

"I want to take you away from all this." Alex kept the smile glued to his lips. He was determined to charm her, but Elizabeth was in no mood to play his little game.

"I have too much to do to play word games, Alex. Go find someone else to play with." Elizabeth picked up a file and began to read.

"Don't ignore me, Elizabeth. I'm trying to give you a break. Come on. Let's go out to lunch. You'll feel better after a nice, hot meal." The smile was still in place, but so was her attitude.

"Go out? Why would I want to go out in this mess?" She pointed out the window at the rain and fog. "I'd rather stay in and work."

"Well, then let me order in and we can eat in my office where it's nice and quiet. That way you won't have to look at all this." He waved his arm over her stacks of files.

"That won't make it go away."

"Come on. Once you get away from your desk, you'll feel different."

"No. I won't." She thumped the file down in frustration. "Can't you see I'm not in the mood for company, especially your company." Her lips were set in a firm line and his smile faded.

"I see. Well, have a good lunch." Elizabeth wasn't sure, but she thought she detected a hint of anger in his voice. She had finally broken that cool exterior. Her satisfaction was soon followed by a feeling of regret. It wasn't like her to goad people that way. It definitely wasn't very Christian-like. She sighed and picked up the next stack of files, too weary to worry about lunch.

She worked with almost no breaks, and by the end of the day she felt mentally and physically exhausted. She had managed to take care of the most critical problems, but there remained a thick stack to do for tomorrow. As she was shutting down the computer system to leave, Alex's private secretary came into her office.

"Hi, Janice. I was just about to leave."

"I'm glad I caught you, Elizabeth. Alex needs the files on the Brennan case. The judge's office called—they moved up the court date. Alex is at home; he asked that you bring all your notes so that the two of you can go over everything tonight."

"Tonight. Can't we do it tomorrow?" The last thing she needed was more work, and the thought of having to deal with Alex made her feel suddenly ill.

"No. The court date has been moved up for Friday. He's going to have to work through tonight and tomorrow just to be ready for opening statements." Janice gave her a sympathetic smile. "I'm sorry, but I'm just the messenger."

"I know, Janice. Thanks for coming down to tell me. I know you're going to be put behind schedule too. I'll see you tomorrow."

"Bye." Janice left, and Elizabeth pulled the Brennan files. Luckily, she had finished her research before the computers slowed down. She put them in her briefcase and grabbed her coat with a sigh.

All the way to Alex's house, Elizabeth complained to God. *Why tonight? Why this weather? Haven't I had enough problems today?* No answer seemed forthcoming, but then again she hadn't stopped long enough to listen for one. She pulled up in front and was startled by the sheer size of the house. She knew Alex lived alone; so why did he need such a big house? The doorbell was answered by a maid, and she was shown into the foyer where the maid took her coat and dripping umbrella.

She looked around at the curved staircase rising up to the second floor. There was a Persian rug, thick and plush, on the hallway floor. Elizabeth carefully wiped her feet on the mat in the foyer before stepping into its luxurious depths. She glanced to the left through an open doorway into a large sitting room filled with Queen Anne furniture and collectibles. The door to the right was closed. She didn't have much time to look around before Alex appeared from a door at the end of the hall.

"Thanks for coming, Elizabeth. I know you've had a long day and the weather is terrible. Why don't you come into my office." He led the way into a room that could only be described as a library. Floor-to-ceiling bookshelves lined two walls, broken on one side by a fireplace with a warm glow coming from a roaring fire. Around the hearth were two wingback chairs and a small sofa. Alex pointed toward one.

"Have a seat by the fire."

"Thanks." She had lost all the fight from earlier today. The warmth of the fire and peaceful surroundings were beginning to work on her attitude. Then she remembered why she had come. "Here is all the information I could find for the Brennan case." She pulled the stack of files from her briefcase. Alex took them and laid them on the cherry desk behind him. It was so large, someone could take a nap on the thing. She almost spoke the thought, but managed to catch herself in time.

"You look pale, Elizabeth. Are you feeling all right?" His solicitous attitude took her by surprise. She was beginning to feel the effects of no lunch.

"I'm okay. I didn't stop for lunch today, so I'm a little tired."

"Well, then, we'll just have to take care of that." Alex used the intercom on his desk. "Mathilda, there will be two for dinner. We'll take it in the dining room in ten minutes."

"Yes, Mr. McClintock." There was a click on the other end. It seemed everyone jumped when he called. No wonder he was angry at lunch. Elizabeth didn't like the way he assumed she would go along with whatever he asked. Her previous mood of contrition was gone.

"There's no need in taking any trouble. Let's just get to work so I can go home and go to bed." She stood up, but her legs were weak from cold and hunger and wouldn't hold her weight. She started to collapse when Alex reached out and caught her, pulling her close. Part of her enjoyed the warmth of his body and the comforting feeling of his arms around her, but the rest of her rebelled and she tried to pull away.

"Don't be so stubborn, Elizabeth." He held her tight and she was too weak and tired to pull away. "Be reasonable. Have some dinner and rest a little while. Then we can get some work done." His arguments were logical, as they always were, otherwise she would have continued to argue. She knew that if she didn't eat soon, she would never be able to finish the job.

"All right."

"That's better." Alex was all charm and smiles again. He

held her for a moment longer and then helped her to the couch. He reached down and pulled off her shoes.

"What are you doing?"

"Taking your shoes so you can't run away." She started to protest until she saw the gleam of humor in his eyes. "I'm just trying to make you comfortable. Your feet are damp." He pulled an afghan from the back and wrapped it around her feet and legs. She leaned back on the sofa and closed her eyes for a moment. She felt warm and pampered and soon drifted off to sleep.

⊱

Alex watched her sleeping from his desk. She was rather lovely. He couldn't wait to get her into bed, but tonight wasn't the night. He'd have to move very slowly with her. Make her feel safe and comfortable. Then he would make his move. Her stubborn will made him want her all the more, although her silly ideas about sex and religion left him cold. Yes, once was all he needed. One night with her would be the cure for his obsession. All he wanted was for her to ask him to make love to her to fill his lust, and he would be through with her. She was just like the other women he had known.

Just then her eyes opened. He put on his most charming and concerned smile. "Did you have a nice nap?" She smiled. "Then let's have dinner."

⊱

After dinner, Elizabeth felt her strength return. That nap and the food had done wonders. Alex had catered to her every need during dinner and she was basking in the warmth of his attentions. They returned to the study, sitting on the couch in front of the fire. The work went quickly, and she felt a pang of regret. It had been such a nice evening that she hated for it to end.

"Well, I guess that's all," Alex said, closing the last file.

"Good," she said. "I guess I should be going now."

"I suppose so. I have a lot of work to finish before Friday."

"Thanks for dinner." She turned to gather her things and remembered she didn't have her shoes. She laughed. "I guess shoes would be good."

"I'm sorry." He laughed as he walked over to the fireplace where he had left them drying on the hearth. "Here they are." She reached for them, but he stopped her. "Allow me, Cinderella. You can't run off without your shoes tonight. You might catch a cold."

"Thank you, kind sir." She gave a mock curtsy. "I'm ever so grateful."

"The pleasure was all mine." He gave a deep bow and kissed her hand. The gesture was so quick and natural that she was taken by surprise. "Let me walk you to your car."

"That won't be necessary. It's nasty out there. There's no sense in both of us getting wet."

"I don't mind." He put a hand under her elbow and escorted her to the foyer. He helped her with her coat, pulling it snug under her chin, and holding the ends a few moments, looking into her eyes. She held her breath waiting for his kiss. Instead, he tucked her under the chin and opened the door. "Ready?"

"Yes." She stammered, taken aback by the sudden change. He opened a large umbrella that was leaning against the wall and walked her to her car.

"Good night, Elizabeth. See you tomorrow."

"Good night." He closed the door and she started the engine. Driving home, she wondered if maybe she had mis-judged him. Something deep within her questioned his motives. Was he really interested in her, and trying to make up for the other night? Or was he only in it for the challenge? Remembering the way he had taken care of her and the feel of his arms, she leaned toward the first.

≈

Alex watched her car pull away, and then he returned to the house. He shook out the umbrella and left it to drain in the foyer. Mathilda would clean it up in the morning. He sat at his desk for a few moments and smiled. He had held himself in check. Although he had wanted to kiss her, he had waited. She would begin to trust him now. She had wanted to be kissed. He could sense it in the way she held her breath and the look in her eyes. He would make her want it even more. His smile widened. He was well on his way to victory. It wouldn't be long now. This was going to be easier than he thought.

six

Elizabeth awoke to the sun peeking through the blinds. She sighed and stretched in the warmth of the covers for one long moment before she threw them back. The shower would be warm and cozy, but the hardwood floors between here and there were cold. She needed some slippers. She dashed for the rug in the bathroom with only her toes touching the icy floor. The steam from the shower soon penetrated the chill of the bathroom, and Elizabeth found herself reluctant to leave the warmth of the spray. She let the pulse pound on her neck and shoulders as she thought about last night. A smile crept around the edges of her lips, but she shook it off. It was nice to be pampered, but Alex was not the right kind of man for her. She headed for her favorite chair for her quiet time and tucked her feet under her. She opened her Bible to the ribbon marker at Isaiah Chapter 40. She read of how the Lord is never weary and is always listening to our prayers. Her eyes fell on the last verse.

"But they that wait upon the LORD shall renew their strength; they shall mount up with wings as eagles; they shall run, and not be weary; and they shall walk, and not faint."

She felt a peace in her soul as she read the words. God had not forgotten her prayer for a Christian man. He would provide it in his own time. She offered a prayer of thanks and then prepared for work with a renewed spirit.

At work, Elizabeth found that the spark of energy had returned, and she set to work. By eleven-thirty she had completed Scott McClintock's research and had the report ready. She found the note with his number and called his office, only to find that he was at home; so she tried the other number. He answered on the first ring, causing her heart to pound.

"Hello, Scott. This is Elizabeth Jordan."

"Oh hi, Elizabeth." He sounded suddenly brighter.

"I just called to tell you that I finished the research. Where would you like me to send it? Or would you prefer to pick it up?"

"Actually, I hadn't planned to come into town the rest of the week. There are some repairs I need to finish here. I guess you could Fed Ex it here, but I'd really like to look at them tonight."

"Oh, well I'll do whatever you think is best."

"What time is it?" The question took her off guard.

"Eleven-thirty. Why?"

"What are you doing for lunch?"

"Lunch? Oh, I hadn't thought about it."

"Well, why don't you come to my house for lunch. I'll clear it with Dad. Consider it a business lunch."

"I guess that would be all right, if it's all right with Mr. McClintock."

"Good, then we'll call it settled. I'll ring Dad and then call you right back." He hung up, and as she placed the receiver on the hook she felt unreasonably happy to be having lunch with Scott, even a business lunch.

As promised, he called back, confirmed the lunch, and gave her directions to his house. He lived near Cedar Heights Community Church, not far from her friends Hope and Jeff. She gathered up the papers and headed for the car. She sang along with the radio, tapping her hands on the steering wheel as she made her way out of the city traffic into the suburbs. His directions were easy to follow, and she soon pulled into a long driveway. This was no house. This was more like a ranch. The drive wound around to the back of an old Victorian-style house with a wrap-around porch. She smiled at the sight of a swing hanging near the corner. There were two buildings in the distance. One was obviously a barn, but she couldn't figure out what the other building was. As she stepped from the car, she was greeted by a large collie.

"Hey, Lady, come here and leave Elizabeth alone." Scott

called from the back door. The dog bounded over to Scott and stood by his side.

"Oh, she's beautiful. I always wanted a dog like her ever since I saw 'Lassie.' Come here, puppy." She knelt down and stroked the dog while talking in low tones. The dog responded by licking her face.

"Lady. Stop that!" Scott reprimanded.

"It's okay," Elizabeth managed between fits of laughter, "I haven't had a dog to do that in ages. I love big dogs."

"Well, I guess you got your dessert before lunch." They both laughed. Scott held the door open and motioned her inside.

The kitchen was large with a breakfast nook in one corner. The walls and floors were done in various shades and prints of country blue and all the appliances were bright white. There were homemade rugs on the floor and crosstitch samplers on the walls. She felt immediately at home.

"Lunch will be ready in about twenty minutes. Why don't we go into the living room."

"Lead the way." She followed him down a long hallway, similar to the one in Alex's house, but the Persian rugs in this hallway looked made for walking on.

"Have a seat."

There was a fire crackling in the fireplace, the light reflected off the marble hearth. Elizabeth sank into a chair facing the fire and watched the firelight flicker on the ships-in-a-bottle on the mantel. The room was filled with beautiful furniture that was neither feminine nor manly. There were Queen Anne sofas in a small grouping to the right and two wingback chairs with reading lamps in another corner. The chair she was sitting in matched the one across from it and a sofa and love seat completed the grouping around the fireplace. It was a big room, but it seemed cozy.

"Want a Dr. Pepper?" Scott called from the kitchen.

"Love one."

He brought in two cans and then sat in the chair opposite her. He propped his feet on the footstool, something Alex would never do.

"You have a nice place."

"I call it home."

"Oh, I almost forgot why I came." She reached in her briefcase and pulled out the report.

"You mean you didn't come for my cooking?" he asked as he took the report.

"Cooking? You mean you cook your own meals?" Her eyebrows raised, and she stifled a laugh at the mental picture of Scott in an apron.

"What's so funny? Don't you think I can cook? I'll have you know I'm a pretty good cook. . .as long as it comes in a can." They both laughed. "Actually, I do have a lady who comes by once a week to do some cleaning and occasionally she has pity on me and leaves me things in the freezer. Which leads me to two important questions."

"What are they?"

"Can you cook?" Before she could protest, he held up his hands. "I only ask because I'm a lousy cook and when I meet a lady I always have to ask."

"The answer is yes, I can cook."

"Great. Now the second question, can you cook well?"

"Yes. You can ask any of my friends. I've been cooking since I was ten."

"Very good. Now I can relax." He gave a mock sigh and leaned back in his chair.

"I'm very happy for you." Elizabeth tried to look offended, but couldn't hide the laughter. "At least you're honest."

"Thank you very much." He slapped his thigh. "I almost forgot lunch." He jumped up and ran into the kitchen and she followed him.

"What's for lunch, anyway?" she asked.

"Lasagna. Don't look so surprised. Mrs. Delaney left it in my refrigerator this morning with cooking directions."

"Thank goodness for Mrs. Delaney. I love Italian food."

"You do? Me too. I just love food in general."

"Well, that makes two of us. Here let me help you with

that." Together they set the table.

"I always pray before meals, will you join me?" He held out his hand. She took it and bowed her head. This was a first. Never in her life had a man ever prayed before lunch or dinner or any meal. She was gaining respect for Scott with every moment.

Over lunch they discussed everything from the state of the American school system to personal preferences. Scott was so easy to talk to that she found herself sharing about her spiritual walk and how she hadn't been to church regularly since she graduated from college.

"Well, you know, it's easy to get out of the habit. You miss once or twice or you move and just don't go looking for a new place," Scott said. She felt refreshed at his lack of the judgmental attitude she usually got from members at her old church.

"I know. I really would like to find a good church. I miss having Christian friends to talk to and discuss the Bible with. Just people who understand how I feel."

"You're more than welcome to come to our church, and it's not like you don't know anybody. You know me and I'll introduce you to our class. I think you'll really like them."

"I might just do that."

"Good. Sunday school starts at ten o'clock." He pushed back from the table. "I guess I'd better clean up this mess."

"Here, let me help you." They cleaned up and loaded the dishwasher. All too soon she was on her way back to work. Despite the prospect of going back to the office, Elizabeth felt lighthearted for the first time in a long while. She burst into a song of praise whose verses lasted until she pulled into the parking lot. She knew that what she had been missing was the fellowship of other Christians. Being with Scott had been like a refreshing breeze after a long drought. Not only because Scott was a handsome guy, but also because he shared her beliefs. She resolved to go to church on Sunday. With that thought in mind, she fairly danced into the building.

seven

Friday was going well until a dozen roses appeared on Elizabeth's desk. At first her heart skipped a beat, but soon stuck in her throat when she realized they were from Alex. It was an invitation to go to the symphony, a rare treat for Elizabeth. She was tempted to go, after the way Alex had been acting lately. She shook her head as though it would rid her of her conflicting thoughts. No. She wouldn't go, not after yesterday.

The day passed so quickly that Elizabeth almost missed her lunch. She was rushing out the door when she ran into Alex, literally.

"Whoa there. Where are you off to in such a rush?" He held her firmly while she regained her balance and then slowly released her.

"Lunch. If you'll excuse me, I don't have much time and I have some errands to run." The words came out in one breath.

"You'd better slow down and catch your breath. No one will notice if you're a few minutes late today."

"I have a lot of work to do before the weekend." She tried to smile and be friendly, but it was hard to be casual when she felt like a trapped animal.

"Well, take it easy. I don't want anything to happen to my favorite researcher." He smiled and touched her shoulder lightly as he moved down the hall. She sighed in relief.

She managed to swallow a cheeseburger between the dry cleaners and the bank and some fries between there and the post office. She was back at her desk and immersed in work in less than an hour, a record. She alternated between her desk and the library the rest of the day, hoping she wouldn't bump into Alex again. She didn't know what to say, but she did know that she couldn't go out with Alex anymore. For one thing, he was not interested in church. For another, she really liked his younger brother. She dreaded what was certain to be a confrontation, and she didn't have long to wait.

"I see you got the flowers."

"Alex." Elizabeth jumped upsetting her coffee mug.

"I didn't mean to scare you. Here let me help." He pulled out a handkerchief and started swabbing the desk.

"It's okay. There wasn't much coffee left. I didn't hear you come in."

"That's because you were buried in your work, literally." A half-smile lifted the corners of his mouth and his eyes twinkled. He pointed to the stacks of files on either side of her.

"Oh, I was just getting these ready to file away. I'm almost finished."

"Good. Then you'll be free this weekend." He spoke as if the matter were settled.

"Actually, I'm going to be busy," she lied. "I have a lot of things to do at home this weekend." She tried to keep her voice even.

"Oh, that's too bad. I was looking forward to taking you to the symphony. Are you sure you can't take out a little time from your hectic schedule." He put his hands on her desk and leaned forward. That ever ready smile and the sheer force of his presence set her nerves on edge.

"I'm sorry. . .I. . .can't." She stumbled over the words, getting up to break the spell he seemed to be casting. "I really have too much to do." He straightened up, and she expected to hear an argument.

"Well, maybe another time. Don't work too hard." His smile lost some of its sparkle, but he left without another word.

Elizabeth was shocked that he had given up so quickly, but she was also relieved. Maybe he had taken the hint, but something told her she hadn't seen the last of him. She put away the stack of files, except for the research for Senator Riggs.

Stuffing the file in her briefcase, she headed for the door. The weekend would be slow, and she could finish the report on her computer at home. She winced as she remembered telling Alex she would be too busy to go out with him. It was too late to think about it now. The damage was done.

The weekend went by slowly. She really didn't have much to do. Cleaning the house took only a few hours and the shopping took even less. After lunch, she sat down and turned on the television. Thirty minutes of channel surfing proved that no matter how many channels she had there was still nothing good on. She wandered around the house, going from room to room searching for something to do. She picked up books only to lay them down and then picked up projects only to grow bored. Her mind was filled with thoughts of Scott and Alex. Alex was every girl's dream for a boyfriend. He was charming, handsome, rich, and attentive, but something about him set warning bells off. He was too perfect, but maybe she was misjudging him. She liked Scott too, but was he interested? She groaned and hit the pillow, willing it all to go away. Finally, it was late enough to go to bed. As she snuggled down in the covers, she knew she had to go to church tomorrow. She needed all the help she could get. With that decision made, she fell into a peaceful sleep.

With a mixture of excitement and nervous energy, she got ready for church Sunday morning. She wanted to look good, but her hair and makeup seemed to have other ideas. Nothing went right. At nine-thirty she rushed out to the car feeling unattractive, but it was too late now. She barely had enough time to get to church. She pulled into the parking lot with five minutes to spare and was surprised to see Scott standing next to his car. She relaxed and waved at him. She hadn't realized how wound up and worried she was about walking into the church alone until she had seen Scott waiting for her.

"I was hoping you would come today," Scott called. He walked over and helped her out of the car.

"You don't know how glad I am to see you. I'm always

nervous going to someplace new."

"I know it can be awkward the first time, so I thought I would wait for a few minutes out here. Let's go on inside." He led her in a side door and down a hallway lined with classrooms, each with a shingle proclaiming the class's title. He led her into the one marked "Singles."

"Elizabeth, I'd like you to meet Mark, David, Rita, Joanne, and Kevin."

"Hi, Elizabeth."

"Nice to meet you."

The voices and faces all blended together, and there was a general blur of introductions and greetings. Elizabeth was sure she'd never remember all the names. Just then the teacher came in and Elizabeth was introduced again. Class was opened with prayer, and in that quiet moment Elizabeth felt the fellowship she had been missing. She relaxed and was soon engrossed in the conversation. The topic was being content in any circumstance, and Elizabeth felt God speaking to her through the lesson. Afterwards, everyone mingled around talking and even hugging.

"Mr. Sparks, I just wanted to tell you how much I enjoyed the lesson. I haven't heard this kind of teaching in a long time." Elizabeth held out her hand, and he gave it a gentle squeeze.

"I'm glad, but my name is James."

"James. Thanks again."

"It was my pleasure. Believe it or not, I get more out of the lessons than you do."

"I find that hard to believe, but I'll take your word for it." Elizabeth smiled at him and then followed Scott to the door.

"We hope you can join us again, preferably next Sunday," James called after her.

"I'll do my best." She smiled and joined Scott in the corridor. "I'm glad you invited me."

"I'm glad you came. Come on. Let's go into the sanctuary." The corridor ended at a set of double doors which led into an auditorium.

Elizabeth looked around at the oak pews highlighted by sunlight streaming through the stained-glass windows. They seemed to glow with an unearthly light. Each window was a different scene from the life of Jesus. To her right was Jesus in the Garden of Gethsemane done in striking detail and color. "It's beautiful."

"Thank you. We just finished it last year. Everyone in the church had a vote in how we decorated and built the church." Scott pointed to the thick blue carpet. "That was the hardest thing to choose."

They moved on into the room and sat down in a pew to the right of the pulpit. The choir sang some upbeat praise songs, and the music minister made some jokes to loosen everyone up. Just before the sermon, a young girl performed a beautiful rendition of "The Via Dolorosa" and hush fell over the audience. The pastor moved to the pulpit and opened his Bible.

"My Scripture text for today is 2 Corinithians 6:14; 'Be ye not unequally yoked together with unbelievers: for what fellowship hath righteousness with unrighteousness? and what communion hath light with darkness?'

"I want us to look at our relationships and see if we have yoked ourselves with darkness. Have you joined your soul with one who doesn't believe in God or who doesn't believe the same as you? If so, you are walking down a dangerous path."

The sermon continued, but Elizabeth's mind was stuck on that one thought. Her mind immediately went to her relationship with Alex. She didn't hear the rest of the sermon as she pondered the pastor's words. Her heart lifted a silent prayer of repentance, and she resolved to stand her ground with Alex. She turned her attention back to the service.

When the last hymn was sung and the last amen spoken, Scott turned, his head cocked to one side. "What did you think?"

"I really enjoyed myself. I needed this so much. I want to thank you for inviting me today." He smiled at her response and relaxed.

"Good. The pleasure was all mine. Now, why don't we see if we can find something to eat. I don't know about you, but I'm starving."

"Me, too. What did you have in mind?"

"How about Chinese? There's a great little restaurant down the road."

"What's the name?"

"McClintock's." He smiled as her eyebrows raised. "Are you questioning my ability to cook, again?" he said with mock seriousness.

"To be honest. . .yes."

"Smart woman. I like that. I'll show you what I mean."

Elizabeth followed him back to the house and was greeted by Lady. She patted the dog on the head and followed Scott into the kitchen, her curiosity at high tide. He motioned for her to come to the refrigerator and pointed to the top shelf. Elizabeth had to laugh. Sitting in full view were three containers bearing the name "Mr. Wong's Chinese Restaurant."

"I like a man who knows how to use leftovers."

He grinned and laughed. Together they set the table and heated up sweet 'n' sour chicken, egg drop soup, and some fried rice. They passed the meal with small talk and a lot of laughter. Elizabeth couldn't remember having such a good time.

"Let's go into the living room for coffee or do you prefer Dr. Pepper?" Scott asked with his hand on the coffeepot.

"Actually, Dr. Pepper sounds great."

"Good. 'Cause I really didn't want coffee." He grabbed two cans from the refrigerator and started to hand her one of them. "Where are my manners? Would you like a glass with some ice?" He looked so apologetic that she had to laugh.

"No, thank you. I prefer mine straight."

"That's another thing we agree on." He motioned her toward the living room and they spent the afternoon talking about life in general. They both liked animals, living in the country, and eating. Elizabeth had never felt so comfortable around a man before, especially a man she was attracted to.

"It's going to be a great sunset tonight," Scott said as he added wood to the fire.

"How can you tell?"

"Just look out the window." Elizabeth turned and was surprised to see the sun low on the horizon.

"Oh, dear! What time is it?" She looked around for a clock.

"It's four-thirty. The sun goes down early this time of the year."

"I didn't mean to stay so late."

"Don't apologize. I've had a wonderful time. It's not often I meet someone willing to eat leftovers and shoot the breeze."

"I'd better get going."

"Since it's already this late, why don't you stay for the sunset? It's going to be quite a show."

She hesitated to answer. One part of her said she'd stayed too long. The other part didn't want to leave. "I guess I could stay a few more minutes."

"Great. Let's watch it from the swing. Get your coat."

They bundled up and sat in the swing while the sky changed from bright blue to orange to midnight blue. They sat in silence unwilling to break the spell. Finally, Elizabeth moved to go, and Scott stood up and put a hand on her arm.

"I really had a great time today, Elizabeth. Maybe we can do it again sometime." His eyes searched her face.

"I'd love to," she said, and his face relaxed into a smile.

"Let me walk you to the car."

"Okay."

Scott put a hand on her arm as she started to get into the car and he pulled her into his arms and hugged her. Elizabeth was surprised and pleased. She felt so at home in his arms. He squeezed her gently and then let her go.

"See you around, Elizabeth."

"Bye."

As she drove home she kept remembering the feeling of being held in his arms. The smile never left her face. He said he wanted to see her again. Feeling truly happy, she slapped the steering wheel, turned up the radio, and drove home singing.

·

eight

Alex's weekend didn't go very well. He had been sure that Elizabeth would go to the symphony with him. Why had she suddenly changed her attitude? He was sure she was lying about being busy. She wasn't very convincing, and he was hard to fool. Something was most definitely up. He spent all of Saturday rethinking his strategy. He had done well in not showing anger or giving her a hard time. He was sure of that.

Sunday afternoon he received a call from his mother, an invitation to dinner. It would be a nice break. He arrived at seven o'clock and noticed Scott's truck already parked in its usual place. Alex's eyes narrowed, but his expression didn't give away the feelings of resentment that rested just below the surface. He walked toward the house slowly, smoothing his face into a smile.

"Alex!" Katherine McClintock called from the stove. "Welcome home. I was afraid you had forgotten where we lived."

"No, Mother. I've just been busy lately. You can always find me at the office."

"It's not the same and you know it. Now, come over here and give me a hug." Katherine's hugs could not be avoided, but Alex received it with a stiff back. His mother's smile faded a little. "Your brother is in the living room with Dad. Why don't you go on in and join them, while I finish up supper?"

"Yes, Mother."

He found his brother sprawled on the couch next to the elder McClintock. Same as always.

The conversation for the next few minutes was strained, a mixture of the weather and politics, but not too much about politics. That was grounds for a small civil war.

"Dinner's ready," Katherine called from the dining room.

They all trooped in and sat in their usual places. Alex picked up his fork to eat, but his mother stopped him.

"We haven't blessed the food, yet, Alex." Alex put down his fork, while his father prayed the usual prayer.

"Lord, we thank you for your blessings and this food you have provided. Bless this food that it may strengthen us to do your will. Watch over our family and protect us. We ask this in Jesus' name. Amen."

"I don't know why you feel it necessary to thank God for providing the food when you know good and well that it was hard work that put food on this table," Alex pointed out.

"Alex!" his mother's outraged voice filled the room.

"Alex, you know that everything is God's and that we don't have anything that God hasn't given to us," the elder McClintock responded.

"I don't get that. We have a lot of money because we earned it. We went out and worked for it. Why should some being off in space somewhere get all the credit. Everything I have, I worked for."

"Alex, why don't you just drop it," Scott replied. "You know how we feel about God and religion, and we know how you feel. Let's just leave it at that and talk about something else."

"Sure, Golden Boy. Whatever you say." The sarcasm was not evident in his voice, but the words alone said a lot.

The rest of the dinner was passed in small talk about the business and talk of family and friends. Scott helped his mother carry the dishes to the kitchen while their father went to his office to make a phone call. Alex picked up a plate and headed for the kitchen. The door was closed and just as Alex moved to open it, Scott said something that caught his attention.

"Mom, I met the greatest girl the other day. She came to church today and we had a nice afternoon. I've never met someone I felt so comfortable with."

"That's wonderful, Scott. What's her name?"

"Elizabeth Jordan. She works at the firm. Have you met her?"

"No, I don't think so. We'll have to invite her to dinner some time."

"That would be great Mom."

The conversation in the kitchen drifted off to another subject, and Alex quit listening. So that was the problem. He should have known it was Scott. Scott always got everything. Alex's mind drifted back to their childhood. From the day he was born, everything was always about Scott. Scott was the good kid who always did everything right. If he had heard it once, he had heard it a million times: "Why can't you be like your brother?" Scott always got what he wanted, but not this time.

Alex's mind began to turn. How could he get Elizabeth away from Scott? A slow smile spread across his face as he remembered Scott's one weakness: his misplaced faith and a disdain for hypocrites. Alex smoothed the anger from his face and plastered his most charming smile in its place.

"What are you two talking about in here?" Alex asked, coming into the kitchen.

"Just things," Scott replied giving his mother a warning look.

"Oh, in that case, why don't we go in the den and catch up." Scott eyed him cautiously.

"Sure, big brother. Why not."

In the den, Alex sat in a wingback chair near the fireplace, and Scott plopped on the sofa on the opposite side. Alex knew he would have to do this carefully.

"Anything new in the construction business, little brother?"

"Not much. I'm working on some home improvement stuff at the house."

"Really. Been out much?"

"No. Why the sudden interest?"

"What? Do you mean I can't take an interest in my brother's life?" Alex looked genuinely hurt.

"You don't usually. What's up?"

"Well, I just wanted to share, that's all."

"Okay, Alex. What do you want to gloat about this time."

"I'm hurt that you would think that I would gloat about anything, but I do have some news I'd like to share."

"So? Out with it."

"I met a woman that I really like."

"What's new about that. You've liked a lot of women."

"This one's different. I might even think of marrying this one." Alex leaned back in his chair. "She doesn't look like a model or anything, but she does have other, shall we say, abilities." The smirk told Scott exactly what those "abilities" were.

"That's more than I wanted to know, Alex. But at least your thinking of doing the right thing."

"Don't you even want to know the name of your possible sister-in-law?"

"Sure, why not?"

"Her name is Elizabeth. She works at the firm. You met her, didn't you?"

The look of shock spread across Scott's face, and Alex knew a moment of triumph. Finally, Scott was feeling what Alex had felt for all those years. Scott quickly tried to cover up his surprise.

"Yes, I did. She helped me do some research."

"You look a little surprised, brother dear. Something wrong?"

"She just didn't seem your type, Alex. She seems a little reserved for your tastes."

"A few minutes alone and she has no reserve at all." The smirk was back, and Scott looked as if he had been punched in the stomach.

"I'm happy for you, Alex."

"Thanks." Alex decided it was time to leave him alone in his misery. He looked at his watch. "Look at the time! I've got to run. See you later. Hey, maybe we could have lunch sometime. You know. You, me, and Elizabeth."

"Sure." Scott sounded less than convincing.

"Bye, little brother."

"Bye." The last thing Alex saw before he closed the door

was Scott's pained expression. He whistled his way to the car.

ॐ

Scott stood in the middle of the den, feeling as if he might be sick. It couldn't be true. It couldn't happen twice. There was no mistaking that smirk. Alex was famous for his ability to talk women into his bedroom. How could he have misjudged Elizabeth? He thought back on the day and wondered how she could sit in church knowing the kind of life she was living? *How could she flirt with me, knowing she was sleeping with my brother?*

Then his mind drifted back to that day four years earlier when he had found Jennifer with another guy. She had seemed so nice. She went to church with him and talked about how she wanted to have a family and live in the country where they could raise their children, go to church together. They had dated for six months, and he was looking at rings. One day, she had canceled their date, saying she was sick; so, he decided to go over and take care of her. The door was unlocked when he arrived, so he went in, only to find her in the arms of another man. She had cried at first, trying to convince him that it was a mistake. When that didn't work, he saw a side of her he had never seen before. She became a horrible person who spat obscenities at him and said he wasn't a real man. If he were a real man, she wouldn't have had to find someone else. He had sworn he would never be fooled again.

As he drove home from his parents', Alex's voice echoed in his ears and the smirk on his face filled his vision. Once more, Alex had managed to ruin something special.

nine

The shrill ring of the telephone woke Scott from a restless sleep. He rolled over and looked at the clock. 4:00 A.M. He groaned and reached for the phone.

"Hello?"

"Hello, Scott. Did I wake you up?"

"Alex? Do you know what time it is?"

"I know it's early, but I need a favor. Are you still going to pick up Claire Bowden at the airport this morning?"

"Yeah, but not till ten o'clock. What's so important that you have to wake me up at four o'clock in the morning?" The irritation in Scott's voice was obvious.

"Well, I have a nine o'clock flight to Chicago for a meeting with the senator, and my car needs to be serviced while I'm gone. I thought since you needed to go to the airport anyway you could follow me to the garage and then drive me to the airport."

"You woke me up before dawn to ask a favor? Big brother, you are pushing the limits of family courtesy."

"Sorry, but I didn't know that my car needed to be serviced until I was driving home last night. I figured you'd be up anyway. I thought construction workers got up with the sun?"

"For your information, the sun is not up yet."

"Well, will you do it?"

"I might as well since I'm up now."

"Thanks, Golden Boy."

"Don't push your luck." Scott hung up the receiver with a bang. Sometimes he wondered why he did anything for Alex. He reached for his Bible and it fell open to Matthew where he had been reading yesterday. Jesus said to treat others the way he would want to be treated, but sometimes he'd rather hit

Alex than hug him. He just didn't understand why Alex behaved the way he did. With a sigh, Scott lifted Alex to the Lord—he knew God could do a lot more for Alex than he could.

Scott went through his morning routine a little faster than normal. Alex had a way of messing up a perfectly good day. Scott tried to regain his normally pleasant demeanor, but found himself slamming doors as he reviewed his conversation of the previous day with Alex over and over again. To top it off, he had to dress up. He hated wearing ties, but he didn't want Claire Bowden to think he was unprofessional. He opted for casual pants and shirt with a tie and a leather jacket. No need to be too professional. He took one last look in the mirror and ran his fingers through his thick, dark hair and then headed for the garage. He patted the truck on his way to the car. He slid the seat all the way back and glanced longingly at the truck. Shaking his head, he started the engine and headed for Alex's house.

❧

Across the city, another phone rang in the early morning stillness. Elizabeth rolled over and ignored the sound. It rang again. On the third ring, she answered the phone in her sleep.

"Hello."

"Hello, Elizabeth. Are you awake?" The sound of Alex's voice jerked her into reality.

"I am now. What time is it?"

"It's about four-thirty."

"Four-thirty? Is something wrong?" Elizabeth's mind quickly jumped to a worst-case scenario. "Is something wrong with your father?"

"No. Relax. I just need a favor." Alex laughed. His obvious lack of regret for waking her up did nothing for her attitude.

"What do you want, Alex?"

"Remember the research you did for the senator?"

"Yeah."

"Where did you put it? I brought it home to finish over the weekend because you said you needed it today."

"I do need it today. I have a nine o'clock flight to Chicago for a meeting with the senator."

"Oh." Elizabeth put her hand to her forehead as if it would help solve the delimma.

"Oh, is right. Is there anyway you could bring it over to my house in the next hour?"

"Yes. It'll take me a few minutes to get ready."

"Good. Then, I'll see you within the hour." He hung up the telephone before she could say good-bye. She mumbled about how ungrateful he was and how inconsiderate he was as she made her way to the shower. She was slow in getting started and when she glanced at her Bible on the nightstand she shook her head. She didn't have time this morning. Her new resolution for daily Bible study would have to wait for another morning. She jerked on some jeans and a T-shirt and brushed her hair. She would have to come back to finish getting ready for work. She grabbed her briefcase, checking to make sure the information was inside before she rushed out the door.

&

Alex hung up the phone with a smile. Everything was going as planned. Elizabeth should arrive within the hour and park in front. Scott would arrive not long after that and park around at the garage. It was perfect.

&

Scott pulled his car in behind Alex's in the rear driveway. He tried the back door, but it was locked. As he started around the corner, the front door opened. Scott slipped into the shadow of the oak tree. His throat constricted. Coming out of Alex's house at 5:15 A.M. was a rather disheveled Elizabeth. He watched as she hurried to her car. He waited until her car was well out of sight and Alex had gone in before he moved from his hiding place.

Alex's housekeeper answered the door and ushered him into the sitting room. He perched on the Queen Anne sofa and tried to sort out what he had just seen. A few minutes later he was still sitting in a daze when Alex came in with suitcase in hand.

"Perfect timing, Golden Boy." Scott jerked at the sound of Alex's voice and then scrambled to act normal.

"I try."

"Did you park in front of the garage?"

"Of course. I always park in front of the garage."

"Just checking." Alex smiled, making Scott feel uneasy. "Well, let's go."

Scott followed Alex to an expensive uptown garage where they left Alex's Mercedes. Then they drove to the Baltimore Washington International Airport. Neither brother spoke until they arrived.

"Thanks for the lift, Golden Boy." Alex retrieved his luggage from the back seat.

"Stop calling me that."

"What?"

"You know what."

"It's just a nickname, little brother. Ease up."

"Well, I don't like it."

"I'll try to remember that."

"See that you do."

Alex inclined his head to the right and shrugged his shoulders before heading in the direction of departures. Scott moved toward the sign marked arrivals. There was no need to hurry. Claire Bowden's flight didn't arrive until ten. He checked the screen to make sure it was on time and then headed for the coffee vendor.

&

Alex whistled as he waited in line and greeted the counter clerk with his most charming smile.

"Can I help you, sir?"

"I just need to check-in." Alex handed her his ticket and watched her pull up the information. She smiled up at him as she worked. He made a mental note of her name, and she handed him his boarding pass.

"Thanks, Carly."

"You're welcome, Mr. McClintock." She gave him a knowing look.

"Call me Alex."

"Okay, Alex. Your flight is boarding now. Let me know if I can be of any assistance at all." She slid a business card over the counter. Alex picked it up. Her home phone number had been written in ink on the back.

"I'll be sure to do that." He smiled and pocketed the card. He whistled his way to the plane. Things were definitely going better than planned.

❧

Scott drank his coffee. He still had thirty minutes to kill. He made his way through the metal detectors and took a chair in the waiting area, where he twisted and turned in his chair, unable to get comfortable. Finally, he stood near the exit door, leaning against the wall.

When the passengers began to file out, he had no trouble spotting Claire Bowden. She was model-tall and thin, with blond hair cut in a short, modern style. She waved and he nodded, and for the first time that morning, he smiled.

"Hi, Scott."

"Hello, Claire. How was your flight?"

"Long. I hope I didn't cause any inconvenience."

"Of course not. I had to drop my brother off anyway. Now, let's get your luggage and get out of here."

"I'm right behind you."

Fifteen minutes later the luggage was stowed and they were on their way to the hotel. He carried her bags in and stood beside her as she signed her name and address. She picked up the key as the bell-hop picked up her luggage.

"I'll let you get settled in, and then I'll come by and take you to lunch around noon. How's that sound?"

"That sounds great. I'll see you then." Scott snapped his fingers and turned back.

"Before I forget, would you like to come to church with me on Wednesday night. We're having a Bible study and then the singles are having a get together of sorts."

"Sounds like fun. I'd love to."

"Great. I'll see you at lunch." Scott waved and then headed

for his car. He pointed the car toward his office and got his mind back on business where it was supposed to be. He wouldn't think about Elizabeth.

ॐ

Elizabeth left Alex's house at 5:15 and hurried back to her apartment. She would have just enough time to get ready, eat breakfast, and get to work on time. Alex had a way of making her life too complicated.

She made it to what should have been her desk just before eight. What she found was a stack of papers in the general shape of a desk. Her shoulders dropped as she surveyed the mess. But She didn't stand there long. Soon, she was organizing and prioritizing the pool of papers into neat stacks. The next two days went by in a blur of work and hastily eaten dinners. There was no time for thoughts of Alex or Scott.

ten

"Call for you on line five, Elizabeth," Joan called down the hall. Elizabeth headed for the phone on the conference table. She groaned in frustration. She would never get all this work done if people didn't stop calling to see if she was done yet. She yanked the receiver from its holder.

"This is Elizabeth." Her voice was more brusque than professional.

"Hi, Elizabeth. This is Melanie from Cedar Heights Community Church. Did I call at a bad time?" Elizabeth could hear the hesitation in the other woman's voice, and a twinge of guilt pricked at her heart.

"No. It's okay. I thought you were my boss calling to check on my progress. Thanks to them I make very little progress. It's nice to hear from you." Elizabeth emphasized the word *you*, hoping to make up for her rude behavior.

"I know what you mean. My boss does that to me sometimes. But let me get to the point. I don't want to keep you too long. I called because we're having a singles' fellowship after Bible study tonight, and we wanted to invite you."

"Oh. That sounds great. I really enjoyed Sunday."

"I'm glad to hear that. Can you come?"

"Sure. Can I bring anything?"

"No. Everything's taken care of. Just bring yourself and a friend, if you want."

"It'll just be me."

"That's fine. I'll see you tonight. Have a good day, Elizabeth."

"Thanks, I believe I will now. Bye." Elizabeth hung up the phone and felt a surge of new energy. She set about her work with a new attitude. Four hours later, she glanced at the clock and was surprised to see it was almost time to leave. She looked at the stack of finished work on her desk with satisfaction. It didn't take long for her to clean up and put things away. Ten minutes later, she was in her car and headed for home. There was enough time for her to grab a bite to eat, freshen up, and get her Bible before she left for church.

Her excitement rose with each passing mile. Her heart was singing because she knew Scott would be there tonight. She had finally met someone she could really talk to about. . . well, about everything. She sensed his attraction to her as well. It was going to be a great night. Pulling into the parking lot, she chose a space near the end of the building. As she entered the education building, she pushed down the nervous feeling that threatened to overcome her and send her running for home.

"Elizabeth. It's great to see you again." Elizabeth jumped and looked around. "I didn't mean to scare you." It was another member of the class.

"I didn't hear you come in. I guess I'm a little jumpy tonight."

"Hard day at work."

"Yeah. You could say three hard days."

"I know what you mean. I don't know what I would do without these refuelings on Wednesday nights. I don't think I would make it until Sunday without them."

Together they entered the classroom, and Elizabeth didn't feel so overwhelmed. Looking around, she noticed several familiar faces, but she still wasn't sure about some of the names. She was pulled into the group and, to her relief, reintroduced to several people. They were all friendly and she chatted, but kept one eye on the door. Just as everyone was about to take a seat, a beautiful blond walked in followed by Scott. He put his hand on her back and guided her to a chair. Elizabeth's heart stopped for a moment and then began to beat unsteadily.

"Everyone, I'd like you to meet Claire Bowden."

There was a general round of greetings. The whole scene was like a replay of Sunday, except Scott had another woman on his arm. A knot started to form in her stomach as she realized that he was just being friendly last weekend, trying to make her feel at home. She tried to compose her face into a relaxed smile.

She spent the entire Bible study trying to look engrossed in the study. Glancing at the clock on the wall, she caught Scott's profile and her heart jumped in her chest, but he seemed not to even notice that she was there. After the closing prayer, everyone was invited to the dining hall for snacks and fellowship. Elizabeth followed the group, and Melanie dropped into line beside her.

"How's it going?" Elizabeth smiled in relief to see a friendly face.

"It's okay. I'm just a little tired."

"This morning it sounded like you were having a tough day." Melanie's eyes crinkled with concern.

"You know how it goes. When it rains, it pours."

They got in line at the snack table, and Elizabeth had to force herself not to turn and stare at Scott. As the night went on, she decided that it wouldn't have mattered anyway. He couldn't see the forest for the trees or should she say tree—all of his attentions were focused on Claire. Elizabeth knew a sharp pang of jealousy. She swallowed it like a pill. Why would he want her when he could have someone as beautiful as Claire?

"Why don't we go over and introduce ourselves to our visitor?" Melanie asked.

"I don't know. I'm still a visitor myself."

"Well that's another good reason to make her feel welcome. Besides, you're not a visitor. Like the pastor says, if you've been here once, you're no longer a visitor."

Elizabeth felt herself being propelled across the room and knew what it must be like to walk to her own execution. She pasted a smile on her face and pulled her shoulders up. If she was going to die, she would do it with grace.

"Hi, Scott. What was your friend's name again?" Melanie's smile was one of genuine welcome.

"Hi, Melanie. This is Claire Bowden. Claire, this is Melanie, an old friend." He smiled and touched Melanie's arm.

"Nice to meet you." Even Claire's voice was beautiful to Elizabeth's ears.

"Nice to meet you, Claire. As for you, Mister," Melanie said, pointing her finger at his nose, "you just watch who you're calling old."

They all laughed, but Elizabeth felt as if she were standing outside looking in a window. Then Melanie pulled her forward.

"Claire, this is one of our new members, Elizabeth Jordan."

"Nice to meet you."

"Hello," was all Elizabeth could manage to push past the lump in her throat. Scott nodded, his only recognition of her presence. Melanie kept the conversation going, asking all the right questions while Elizabeth stood by mute, until Melanie led Claire away on the pretense of showing her the new bride's room, leaving Elizabeth and Scott alone. They stood there for what seemed an eternity until Scott finally broke the silence.

"Did you have a nice weekend?"

"Of course, you should know." She was taken aback by the question, considering she had spent most of the weekend with him.

"Have you seen my brother lately?"

"No. He's on a business trip to Chicago." He looked angry at her reply, but she couldn't think why. He stood there for a few seconds. "I'd better go check on Claire." He strode away, leaving Elizabeth alone in the middle of the room. Feeling conspicuous, she looked around for some means of escape, but everyone seemed involved in their own conversations. She picked up her purse and slipped quietly out the side door.

All the way home, she went over and over the evening in her mind. Her stomach lurched, and her chest felt like lead. She had obviously been mistaken about Scott. He was obviously trying to get rid of her unwanted attentions. Tears threatened to fall, but she held them back. It was her own fault for jumping to conclusions. She must have been crazy to think that he would be interested in her.

Her townhouse seemed lonelier than usual, and she turned on some music to fill the quiet, but nothing sounded right. She flipped through all of her tapes and CDs, but she could still hear and see the whole evening replaying in her mind. Every memory brought a fresh wave of humiliation and pain. It was just like the prom all over again—standing alone in the crowd, looking for somewhere to belong. She had thought she had found it at Cedar Heights but she must have been wrong. She didn't belong anywhere. She tried to push the thoughts aside as she got ready for bed, but the minute she lay down in the darkness, the tears began to flow.

"Oh, God, help me," she whispered. Then the darkness settled.

eleven

Thursday morning Elizabeth looked in the mirror and groaned. Her eyes were red and puffy from crying herself to sleep. She spent an extra ten minutes and an extra layer of makeup trying to cover up her distress. A last look in the mirror told her that the effect was minimal, but she didn't have time to try anything else. When she got to work, she went straight to her office, avoiding the usual morning pleasantries over coffee in the breakroom. She spent the entire morning with her head bent over her work. Thankfully, she was left to herself all morning. But the reprieve was not to last long—just before high noon trouble arrived.

"Hello, Elizabeth."

She didn't have to raise her head to recognize the voice. She kept her head down as she worked. "Hello, Alex."

"Busy?" He sat on the edge of her desk.

"Yes."

"Well, everyone has to take a break for lunch. Boss' orders."

"Which boss?" Elizabeth continued to look at her desk.

"Me. By the way, when the boss speaks you're supposed to pay attention."

"I am paying attention."

"Then stop working and look at me." He reached down and pulled her chin up so that she was looking him in the eye. "Elizabeth, what's wrong?" His voice was filled with a concern that took her by surprise.

"Nothing." She pulled her face away from his hand.

"It looks like something to me, but I won't push. Whatever it is, why don't you come to lunch with me and forget all about it for a while."

"There's nothing to forget. It's just allergies."

"Whatever you say. Let's go to lunch." Alex stood as if to go.

"I'll just order in later." She looked up, her mouth drawn in a firm line.

"Whatever you say." He held his hands palms out and left as quietly as he came.

Elizabeth was surprised that he took the hint so quickly. Maybe she had gotten her point across after all. She was still bent over her work twenty minutes later when Alex's secretary stopped in front of her desk with a take out box.

"What's this?"

"Mr. McClintock told me to bring this to you." She shrugged her shoulders and left.

She opened the box and a delicious aroma filled the office. Sweet 'n' Sour pork and oriental rice with an eggroll, her favorite. Her stomach growled in appreciation. She smiled in spite of her promise never to have anything to do with Alex. Though, it was thoughtful of him.

❧

Back in his office, Alex knew a moment of triumph. From the look on her face, he could tell that Scott had given her the brush off. He sat down in his chair, hands pressed together as if in prayer, but prayer was the last thing on his mind. What would be his next step? He contemplated the question for a few moments. A smile spread across his face as the answer came. He knew exactly what to do.

❧

Friday morning, Elizabeth was surprised to find a sizeable amount of her work missing from her desk and a note saying that the work was being distributed among the other librarians. Her feelings went from relief that some of the pressure was gone, to irritation that someone thought she was incapable of handling it. She marched down the hall to Alex's office, but his secretary was the only one in sight.

"What's going on?"

"I don't know what you mean?

"My work load. What happened?" Elizabeth stood there, her arms folded in a stance that said, "Don't mess with me."

"Oh, that. Alex just said that you looked a little tired yesterday and that you had really too much work for one person. He told me to divy up some of the busywork and leave you with the real research."

"Oh." Elizabeth's arms came down. "Thanks." She started down the hall, but turned back. "I'm sorry I was so rude."

The other woman shrugged her shoulders, and Elizabeth turned back to her office. She sat down at her desk, her mind whirling. Why would Alex do that? She puzzled it over and over, but could find no answer. She couldn't help feeling softer toward Alex. He had been so nice lately. Maybe she should give him another chance, at least be friends. A voice deep inside yelled, *Don't trust him, don't let him near you.* But she pushed the voice down and smothered the sound, turning to her work with a smile.

Elizabeth didn't see Alex all day. She caught herself looking for him and listening for his step in the hallway. Nothing. The rest of the day was spent in finishing up research on several cases. By the end of the day, she had cleaned all the pending cases off her desk and put all the files away. She left the office feeling a mixture of weariness and satisfaction in a job well done.

At home, she changed into jeans and an oversized sweatshirt. Turning on the light in the kitchen, she opened every cabinet and the refrigerator at least twice without finding anything that appealed to her. She was just contemplating ordering in Chinese food when the doorbell rang. Who could that be? She walked to the door, looked through the peephole, and opened the door to find Alex with a bag from Mr. Lee's Chinese Restaurant.

He held up his hands as if to stop a protest. "Before you throw me out, I just came by with a peace offering. It's been a long week, and I thought you might like to share some Chinese food." She opened her mouth to answer, but he silenced her. "The Chinese food is yours automatically. The offer of company is optional."

"Are you through?" she said, her arms folded in front of her chest.

"Yes." He looked like a man waiting for sentencing.

"Then come in before the smell causes me to faint from hunger."

His smile said it all. He jumped through the door and closed it as if afraid she might change her mind. Taking the food into the breakfast nook in the kitchen, they ate and talked like old friends. Then as soon as they had cleaned up the table, he became very serious.

"Elizabeth, we need to talk." He pulled her into the living room and onto the couch, except this time he put a large space between them.

"What?" She looked at him and felt her heart begin to race. There was something in his tone that made her uneasy.

"When I came over here the last time, I was out of line. I shouldn't have pushed the way I did, and I shouldn't have said the things I said. I want to apologize."

Elizabeth just stared. Her mind refused to comprehend or respond. The more she stared, the more downcast his face became. "I guess that means forgiveness is out of the question." It was more a statement than a question, and Elizabeth shook herself from her reverie.

"No. I mean, I forgive you."

"Whew! For a minute there, I thought you were going to hold it against me forever." The charming smile was back, and Elizabeth felt herself smile back. "That's much better. I haven't seen that smile in ages."

"I haven't had a lot to smile about lately."

"Then I guess I'll just have to change that."

❧

His parting words rang in her ears. He seemed so interested in her well-being and her happiness. It was a feeling that she had not known in years. He had invited her to his health club for the day as his visitor, not as his date. She relived the evening over and over again, until she drifted off to sleep.

The next morning she awoke early, anticipating an enjoyable time. She searched through her closet, looking for something chic and slimming which was a hard combination to come by in her wardrobe. She finally settled on a navy-and-white exercise suit that accented her dark hair and eyes and covered those extra pounds. Maybe today she could burn off a few of those. Anything was possible.

Alex dropped by at nine to pick her up. He looked sharp in his designer sportswear. He took in her outfit with a smile. "You look lovely. That color suits you."

She returned the smile and all worries about her appearance faded at his approval. She bounced down the steps to the car, not even noticing the cold air. Alex laughed at her enthusiasm.

"You look like a kid who just found out he's going to the zoo."

"Better than the zoo. I've always wanted to spend the day at one of those health clubs, but when I was in school I couldn't afford it."

"What about now?" he asked as he held the car door open.

She put her arms on the top of the door. "Now, I don't really have any friends who live close enough to go with me, and I never had the nerve to go by myself. I was always envious when I saw people who won those "Queen for a Day" contests on all those talk shows. It sounds like fun."

"Then you shall have it." He closed the door and circled round to the driver's side. "I pronounce you Queen, and today is your day."

"Thank you, kind sir." She gave him a mock bow. She thought he was only being fanciful, but when they arrived at the club she found out differently. He turned her over to one of the trainers and told her he would see her at lunch. She followed the trainer to a room at the end of the hall.

"Mr. McClintock says you are to have a facial, manicure, pedicure and massage before lunch," the trainer informed her.

"A what?"

"The whole works. He said you were. . .what was it. . .oh, queen for the day, and to give you the full treatment at his expense." The trainer smiled, obviously pleased by what would be a sizeable commission.

Elizabeth stuttered, but all her protests were pushed aside. She finally, accepted the gift and enjoyed the whole process. By lunch, she felt like a new person. She found Alex seated at a table on the patio, overlooking a luscious indoor pool.

"Did you have a good time?" Alex asked.

"Marvelous. I feel like a new person."

"I hope not. I'm fond of the old one." Alex smiled at her obvious enjoyment and his eyes roamed, taking in every inch of her. She would do nicely. "What would you like for lunch?"

Lunch was a seafood salad and iced tea which seemed appropriate, because even though it was winter outside, it seemed like perpetual summer in the club. They finished lunch and he took her on a tour of the club, stopping to demonstrate some of the equipment. Alex was stopped several times by other members, and she was introduced to scores of people she would never remember. After that, he showed her how to play tennis. By four o'clock, she was tired, but exhilarated by the day's experiences. She sighed as Alex opened the car door back at her townhouse.

"What was that for?" he questioned.

"Just sad that it's over. I had a really great time."

"I'm glad. Are we friends again?" He held out his hand and tilted his head, trying to look angelic.

She had to laugh. "I guess so."

His faced relaxed into a smile. He wiped his forehead as though wiping off sweat. "Whew! Now we can get on with our lives, starting with tomorrow. What are you doing?"

She frowned. Originally, she had planned to keep attending Cedar Heights, but now she was not so sure. The thought of Scott revived the feeling of pain and humiliation she had managed to keep buried the last few days.

"What's wrong?" he asked, leaning over to touch her arm.

"Oh, I'm just not sure. Some of my plans got changed."

"Does that mean you're free to go to church with me tomorrow?"

"Church?" she asked, totally taken aback by this turn of events.

"Yes, church. Don't look at me like that. I'm not a heathen. I was raised in church." He put a hand to his heart as if her words had wounded him.

"I just never thought you. . .I mean I didn't think. . ." she ground to a halt, unable to save the moment. His laughter at her predicament eased the tension. "I'm sorry, it's just that I never thought of you as the church type."

"I'll forgive you. How about it?"

"Sure. Where do you go to church? "

"Stonehaven Baptist Church. It's near my house. I'll pick you up around nine-thirty. Okay?"

"Okay."

"See you then." He turned and glided down the sidewalk to his car.

"Bye." She raised her hand in a salute before turning and going into the townhouse. He never failed to surprise her.

twelve

Sunday morning, Scott picked up Claire Bowden at her hotel and drove to Cedar Heights. She was her usual charming self and his friends were gracious, but something was missing today. He looked around trying to put his finger on the problem. Something just didn't feel right.

The sermon was taken from Luke 6:37, "Judge not, and ye shall not be judged." Scott squirmed in his seat as thoughts of last weekend flashed before his mind. Unbidden, an image of Elizabeth leaning forward in her seat as if transfixed by the message filled his mind. She seemed so genuine in her desire to be closer to God. Could he have misjudged her? Maybe she had just made a mistake, fallen to temptation? With that thought came the image of her with Alex and something inside twisted in pain. He shook his head trying to loosen the picture from his mind. Claire nudged him with her elbow, and Elizabeth's face faded from view. Everybody was standing up for the invitation. He stood, willing his mind to focus on the pastor. He had to forget both of them.

❧

Elizabeth followed Alex into the largest church she had ever seen in her life. Row upon row of pews lined the long room and overhead she could make out large balconies. Everything from the floor to the pews was covered in a rich red. Elizabeth noted the beautiful cherry pews as she sunk into the luxurious comfort of the seats. The organist was playing a classical piece on the huge pipe organ. The sound reminded her of a funeral.

"What do you think?" Alex whispered in her ear.

"It's beautiful." She smiled and Alex nodded.

The music changed to a sort of march and everyone stood. Looking over her shoulder, Elizabeth was stunned to see the pastor in a flowing robe preceded by the choir.

Leaning over she whispered in Alex's ear, "Is this a special occasion?"

"No. Why do you ask?" He looked puzzled.

"Nothing." She shook her head and watched the processional make its way to the stage. Stage was an apt word. The whole service seemed to be a performance. The music was flawless. The pastor's sermon was a work of art that could have been compared to Shakespeare. The people were all smiles. Everything went smoothly and on time, as printed in the church bulletin. It was all too perfect. Elizabeth's mind went back to the Sunday before with Scott and she sighed.

"Something wrong?" Alex whispered.

"No." She shook her head and then touched a hand to her mouth.

"Up late?" He smiled.

Elizabeth just shook her head in agreement, unwilling to disturb the performance. She gave herself a mental shake. She shouldn't be so judgmental. Maybe she should give it a little time. This type of worship service was new to her.

The rest of the service was much like the beginning. Alex seemed content enough with his arm across the back of the pew and his face turned toward the pastor, drinking in the words. Elizabeth did not feel any strength or sense any new insights from the sermon. They were just pretty words, well spoken.

≈

Alex stretched his arm across the back of the pew, touching her shoulder lightly. He turned his face to the pastor, but he didn't see him. His mind was filled with the picture of Carly from the airport. He had met her for only a moment, but he knew he would call her. She wouldn't be as stiff as this one. He glanced at the woman beside him. Elizabeth would be the perfect society wife. She knew all the right things to say, knew how to impress people. Even his parents would like her. But he had other needs. The image of Carly flashed back on his mind, and Alex spent the rest of the service contemplating how he would spend his evening.

❧

Soon enough the call to stand for the benediction and final prayer came. Then the crowds moved as one toward the door. The pastor and his wife waited at the door to greet everyone, and people filed out as if they were in a receiving line to greet the king and queen. She was surprised to find that the people scattered the moment they got past the door. Within five minutes the whole place was barren. She remembered the fellowship she had had at Cedar Heights and sighed once again.

"You really should go home and take a nap," Alex said. He leaned over and brushed a stray hair out of the way. "Let's get lunch. Okay?"

She nodded her agreement and followed him to the car.

❧

At a little past one, Alex dropped Elizabeth off at her house. Then he drove home to make a phone call. He pulled her business card from his wallet and dialed the number.

"Carly?. . .Yes, it's Alex McClintock. How are you?. . .Up to a drink and maybe a little dancing?. . .Great. I know a little nightclub that I think you'll enjoy. . .Pick you up around eight?. . .See you then."

Alex hung up the phone and then sat down in his desk chair, stretching back. With his hands behind his head, he looked back on the day. Normally, he would have considered a day spent in church a waste, but taking Elizabeth to church had definitely increased his chances. He turned his mind from Elizabeth and focused on Carly and the coming evening.

❧

Elizabeth spent the afternoon and evening channel surfing. She tried to read a book, but nothing she picked up was interesting. Her thoughts turned to Alex. Just when she thought she knew him, she would find out something new. He seemed right at home in church. Then a picture of Scott at church came to her mind. Scott seemed to enjoy his time at church. There was something about the way he looked when he was at church that was missing from Alex. She shook her head. She had to stop comparing the two. They were different people.

☙

Scott took Claire back to her hotel after lunch. She was nice and certainly not hard to look at, but something was missing. He had had the same feeling in church that morning. He sat down in his favorite chair and looked outside. The beauty of nature had never failed to give him a sense of peace, but today, he could find no peace. In his heart, he knew that something was wrong, yet he refused to explore the possibilities. Elizabeth's face filled his mind, and he jumped up from his chair and headed for the barn. He normally didn't work on Sunday, but he couldn't just sit around here. He spent the evening polishing all the saddles until he could see his image in the leather. But he didn't like what he saw. Throwing down the cloth, he moved to another task and another. He fell into bed that night exhausted, but sleep was still slow in coming. His final thought was "judge not, and ye shall not be judged" and a picture of Elizabeth flitting through his dreams.

thirteen

Elizabeth spent November caught in a whirlwind of activity. Alex took her everywhere. It seemed every night was full. A concert here, the ballet there, an art exhibition, or one of an endless string of dinner parties kept her hopping. By the time Thanksgiving approached, she was exhausted, but Alex was already trying to plan their vacation. She didn't even remember when it had become "their" vacation. It was this topic of conversation that gave her a sense of foreboding.

On the Monday before Thanksgiving, Alex dropped by her desk as he often did, but Elizabeth sensed something different in his mood. She put down the folder she was working on and looked up at him.

"Something wrong?" she asked.

"Why do you ask? I haven't even said anything yet." He smiled, but it didn't fool her. For the first time she sensed hesitation on his part.

"Just a feeling."

"Well, I just thought I would come and see where you wanted to go for lunch today."

"You told me last night that you had a lunch meeting today."

"Well, that's off now."

"Canceled?"

"You could say that." Alex tapped his fingers on her desk. "So, where do you want to go for lunch?"

"I had already planned to eat lunch with Morgan."

"Can't you cancel?" His eyes looked clouded, as if he was somewhere else.

"There is something wrong, isn't there?" she prodded.

"I would like to talk with you about something. Can you make other plans with Morgan?"

"Sure." Once assured that she would go with him to lunch, he returned to his office, leaving Elizabeth curious and confused. She turned back to her work, but her mind was still pondering the look on Alex's face.

&

Leaving Elizabeth, Alex returned to his office. He frowned at his reflection in the desktop. The fickleness of women never ceased to amaze him. For the last month, he had showered her with flowers, lingerie, and jewelry, but that wasn't enough. He had spent night after night with her, but she wanted more. He had had to cancel lunch. She wanted to go out with him in public, but he couldn't risk it. He would just have to say good-bye to Carly. Too bad really, she had been a lot of fun. He shook his head in disappointment and then shrugged it off. He picked up the phone.

"Mario?. . .Yes, I'd like a very quiet table for two. . .Yes, that'll do nicely. Good-bye." He hung up the phone with a smile. It was time to move things up a step.

&

Alex was prompt as always, but he seemed preoccupied. He didn't speak all the way to the restaurant, which left Elizabeth with a lot of time to puzzle over his behavior. He took her back to Little Italy, the first place he had ever taken her. They were shown to a table in the corner, almost hidden by some hanging plants and a decorative screen. Alex settled in his chair, taking extra pains with his napkin, before he ever spoke and that was to the waiter.

"We'll have the usual, Antoine." The waiter nodded and backed away from the table in one smooth move. Alex cleared his throat, but didn't say anything.

"Is something wrong?" Elizabeth watched him carefully.

"That's the second time you've asked that question." He smiled as though it was amusing, but something about his tone made her think he was avoiding the question.

"Maybe for good reason." She waited for a response, but he continued to straighten the silverware. "Well?"

"Well, what?" He didn't even look up.

"Is there something wrong?"

"No." His answer was staccato, quick and sharp. Now, she knew there was something going on. His characteristic coolness was warming up. She'd try a new tactic.

"You said you wanted to talk to me. What about?" She tilted her head so that she could better see his face. She put a finger under his chin and lifted until his eyes were level with hers. "I can't see those big brown eyes when you look at the tablecloth."

His face relaxed into a smile, and he took her hand in his, placing a soft kiss on her finger. "You have a very good memory." He leaned back in his chair, still holding her hand. "I do need to ask you a question, but I'm not sure how to go about it."

"Oh?" she answered. Her heart began to beat wildly at the tone of his voice. "What is it?" She was almost afraid to hear what he was going to say.

"We haven't known each other a long time, but I feel as though I've known you all my life. I know that's a cliché, but it's true. I want to be with you in every sense of the word." She opened her mouth, and he held out his palm to silence her. "I know how you feel about that. I'm not trying to pressure you into something." He stopped and hit the table in frustration. "This is not coming out right at all."

"I don't understand. What are you saying?" She watched him, holding her breath.

"I want to be with you because I'm in love with you." She stared, her mind not comprehending. "I want to marry you."

His words were barely uttered before the waiter appeared with their lunch. Elizabeth was grateful for the time to gather her wits. She groped for the right words to answer with, but her wits refused to gather. The waiter disappeared and Alex turned to her, waiting.

"Well. Don't you have anything to say?" He watched her intently, but she just sat there with her lips frozen together.

"I. . .uh. . .I. . .uh. . .I don't know what to say." She finally blurted out.

"I'm not asking you to marry me right away. I just want you to know how I feel." He leaned forward taking both of her hands. "Look, I know this obviously came as a surprise to you." *You bet it did.* "I also realize that you need time to think about what I've said." *No kidding.* "I have an idea."

"What?" She would take anything that would get her out of this situation.

"Why don't we go our separate ways until after Thanksgiving? That way we both can have a little space to think about it."

"I think that's a good idea."

"Then it's settled." He released her hands. "I think we should eat before the food get's cold." She nodded. Elizabeth picked up her fork just to have something to do.

Alex talked about the office and the weather in an obvious attempt to break the tension, but she was relieved when he asked for the check. The ride back to the office was as quiet as the ride there, but for different reasons. This time she was the one who needed to think.

fourteen

Elizabeth spent the next few days in confusion. Alex stayed in his office, and she ate lunch with the girls. At night they went their separate ways. Staying at home every night made Elizabeth aware of how accustomed she was to having someone around. Her work was starting to suffer because she was continually mulling over the situation with Alex. She finally asked for her vacation days to be added to the Thanksgiving holidays. On Friday, she cleaned her office and headed for Hope's. Every year since her parents' accident she had spent the holidays there. This year she had thought she might spend it with Alex's family, but the thought of seeing Scott all weekend made her stomach tie up in knots. In light of the circumstances, she was glad to make a quick getaway. She needed time to think.

Hope was only too glad to have her for the whole week instead of two days. The minute she stepped into the house she felt peace return in a calm wave, washing over her troubled spirit. She slept well that night for the first time in many days.

They spent the next few days cleaning and baking. It was like being roommates again. It had been a long time since she had felt so at home. Since Hope and Stacey had gotten married, these get-togethers had gotten few and far between. She couldn't blame them really. It was the way it was supposed to be. When a woman got married, her husband and then her children became her main priority. It was just hard being the only one without someone.

That thought continued to bounce around in her head all week, until by Thursday it was a staccato drumbeat that threatened to overcome her. Then Hope's family arrived. All her sisters and their husbands and kids filled the house with laughter and conversation. The noise, mixed with that steady drumming in her head, had her searching for aspirin like a drowning man for a lifeline. Hope found her in the kitchen.

"What're you looking for?" Hope asked. Her face all at once concerned.

"Just some aspirin. I have a little headache." Elizabeth tried to smile, hoping to wipe that look of concern off her friend's face. She didn't need any problems today.

"They're on the top shelf in the bathroom."

"Thanks." Hope moved to go get them. "That's okay. I can find them. You've got guests to take care of," Elizabeth insisted.

"Those aren't guests. They're family and they can take care of themselves."

"Meaning I can't?" Elizabeth asked, hands on hips.

"I didn't say that." Hope threw up her hands in defeat. "Go ahead. Fend for yourself."

Hope went back into the dining room and Elizabeth made her way to the bathroom, closing door. The noise below faded to a dull hum. She sighed and leaned against the door, her hand pressed against her temple. Opening the cabinet, she moved the deodorant, shaving cream and finally found the aspirin behind a brush. She laid her head on the cool tile of the bathroom wall. Looking at her watch, she knew if she wasn't back soon, Hope would come looking for her. With a sigh, she headed back downstairs.

Hope outdid herself. There was the traditional turkey, cranberry sauce, and stuffing, plus her famous chocolate mousse and a variety of vegetables. There was so much food that an army couldn't have eaten it all, but everybody did their best to put it away. After the meal, there was a general groan as plates of pumpkin pie, chocolate mousse and carrot cake were pushed away half-eaten. Then a general retreat was sounded as the men headed for the recliners and the women headed for the kitchen.

"Why is it that the women always do all the cooking and the cleanup in this family?" asked Aunt Hilda. "Whatever happened to the women's movement and equality?"

"I don't think it's made it this far, Aunt Hilda," Hope replied from the sink.

"Well I think we ought to start a revolution in this household."

"You'll have to wake the troops first," Hope's mother said, holding the door to the living room open. Laughter filled the room at the sight—the six men lay in varying states of repose, some with mouths open sucking air in and blowing it out. It reminded Elizabeth of a whale she had seen at Seaworld. The women's laughter woke Jeff from a gentle slumber, and he struggled to get off the couch. Beached whales were more graceful.

"What is it?" Jeff asked.

"Aunt Hilda wanted to know why we're all in the kitchen and you guys are all out here." Hope cocked her head, hands on hips, and surveyed the room. "I guess that's pretty obvious."

"What?"

"It's just that, well I hate to say it, but you guys are just more at home in your easy chairs."

"What do you mean by that?"

"Oh, nothing, honey."

"Don't you nothing-honey me, Hope. Are you trying to imply that I," he placed his hands on his chest and then gestured to the other men, "and my comrades here cannot handle the kitchen."

"You said it, not me," Hope replied looking as innocent as a kid with her hand in a cookie jar. She turned and winked at Elizabeth. "What do you think Liz? Could they even find the sink?"

"I don't know, Hope. It might be too difficult for the men." Elizabeth tried to hide a smile.

"What are you giggling at?" Jeff growled at Elizabeth.

"Nothing." Her eyes were large and round, looking the part of the innocent bystander.

"Do you think we're just a bunch of tough guys with no sensitivity? Well, we'll just show you." Jeff stood up and roused each man from his half slumber. Most were totally ignorant of the conversation. "Come on, men. We've been challenged." He lifted his toothpick like a flag before the charge. "Into battle."

In the kitchen, Jeff pulled out one of Hope's daintiest aprons and proceeded to do an immitation of Hope cooking. The other men joined in and soon it was complete chaos in the kitchen.

"That's enough," shouted Jeff above the din of laughter and yelling. "Ladies, out." Jeff held the door open and pointed toward the living room. "You deserve a rest." He bowed at the waist as the women filed past and then closed the door with a flourish. The women sank into the chairs, laughing.

"You got a good man, Hope," Aunt Hilda said, nodding her a head and pointing her finger. "My Douglas would never have gone into the kitchen, not even for a snack. He sent me for the snacks."

"I know, Aunt Hilda. My Jeff's a sweetie. When I had the flu last winter, he brought me breakfast, lunch, and dinner in bed." Hope smiled as she listened to her husband giving orders in the kitchen.

"Now, don't get me wrong. My Douglas was a fine man. He was just a product of his raising. He was my best friend and I miss him. We used to talk about everything." The glow of unshed tears brightened her eyes, and she stopped to dab a handkerchief at the corners.

Elizabeth felt a stab of pain as Aunt Hilda talked. More than anything, that was what she wanted: someone to share things with and talk to, someone to come home to. Tears began to surface and a wave of self-pity rushed over her. She made the excuse of a headache and slipped out of the room, but on her way out she caught Hope's eye as a tear slipped down her cheek.

Elizabeth cried into her pillow, sobs shaking her body, though she made no sound. A bitterness began to envelope her heart as she thought of all her friends who were married and so happy. It wasn't fair. Then she remembered Alex. He wanted her. He said he wanted to marry her. He went to church; he made a good living; he was attractive and attentive. Why shouldn't she marry him? Deep in her soul a voice struggled to cry out, but she silenced it. She got up off the bed and went in the bathroom to splash some cool water on her face. She had made a decision. She looked at herself in the mirror. Somehow she didn't look like a happy bride-to-be. Pushing the thought out of her mind, she thought of Alex as he struggled to share his feelings with her. He loved her and she was attracted to him. He made her feel good about herself. Wasn't that the beginnings of love? Of course. It had to be. She left the room with a sense of relief that a decision had been made.

Later that night, Hope cornered Elizabeth in the now-polished kitchen. "What's wrong?"

"Nothing's wrong."

"Don't give me that. I saw your face this afternoon. Give it up!" Hope had that look on her face, and Elizabeth knew she would have to tell her.

"I just had a lot on my mind and that headache made it hard to think."

"Well, why don't you get it off your mind by telling me?"

"You don't give up, do you?" Elizabeth gave her friend a crooked smile.

"Not when it comes to you, so give!" Hope pulled out a chair and sat down, motioning for her to take the other.

"Last week Alex told me that he wanted to marry me."

It was a good thing Hope was sitting down, because she was obviously shocked. "But you've only known each other a few months."

"Actually, I've been working there for three years," Elizabeth argued.

"You weren't dating then. You hardly ever saw the guy," Hope replied.

"How do you know? You don't work there." Elizabeth was on the defensive. "We've spent a lot of time together in the last several months."

"Enough to know that he's the one you want to spend your life with? Do you really know him?" Hope reached out and touched her hand willing her to answer.

"Of course I know him." Elizabeth brushed away the thought that she had just said that very thing to herself not long ago. "He's sweet, and thoughtful, and attractive. What more could a girl want? And he's very rich." She tacked that on for good measure, but both of them knew that money wasn't the issue.

"Is he a Christian?"

"Yes, he goes to church with me every Sunday."

"Just going to church doesn't make him a Christian, Elizabeth."

"Don't be so judgmental, Hope."

"I'm only trying to make sure you don't make the biggest mistake of your life. There's something about this guy that I don't like."

"How would you know, you've never met him? You only know what I've told you about him." Elizabeth threw her hands up in frustration.

"I know." Hope looked her in the eyes and Elizabeth knew that Hope had a point. Elizabeth lowered her eyes to the table. The silence lasted for several minutes. The ticking of the clock sounded loud in Elizabeth's ears. Finally, Hope spoke, "It's your decision, Elizabeth. I just don't want you to rush into anything." She patted her hand, and then left Elizabeth to her own thoughts.

~

The next day Stacey met them for lunch. She squealed with delight when she heard the news. "You mean that dreamy man really asked you?" Stacey asked her eyes sparkling with excitement.

"Well, he didn't give me a ring or propose formally. He said he wanted to give me time to think about it first."

"What's to think about, honey? He's gorgeous. I've seen him in court and he's a doll." Stacey's excitement was catching.

"He is, isn't he?" Elizabeth smiled. She felt pride rising up as she thought of Alex. She would be Mrs. Alex McClintock.

"I'm sure," Hope replied, but Elizabeth could hear the uncertainty in her voice. Stacey was oblivious.

"Me too. I'm just so excited. We'll have to go shopping. What kind of dress do you want?"

The rest of the lunch was filled with questions from Stacey about bridesmaid dresses and flowers. Elizabeth was overcome with the amount of decisions to be made. Hope sat quietly, entering the conversation with monosyllable replies. Stacey got more excited with the moment, unaware of the tension building at the table. Finally, they all went their separate ways. Elizabeth tried to smile as she waved good-bye to Stacey, but the smile faded when she caught Hope's eye. There was no happiness there, only traces of concern. Elizabeth turned purposefully to her car and set out in search of Alex.

fifteen

Scott pushed away from the table with a groan. Mother always made enough food for an army, even though there was just the four of them. He knew his parents would like grandchildren and were beginning to lose hope. He and Alex were both getting older and neither one seemed intent on getting married, much less having children. Alex least of all. There was a different woman every month, kind of like the flavor of the month at the local frozen yogurt place. He and Alex were opposites. Alex dated hard and Scott hardly dated. His mother and father had instilled in him a desire for a godly woman, one who put God first in her life. Those girls were few and far between these days. So instead of dating, Scott spent his off time working at home or at the church. Glancing in the living room, he saw his mother sitting on the arm of his father's chair. The mere sight of them together stirred the long-buried desire in his heart that grew each day. At the thought of a family, Elizabeth's face popped into view. Elizabeth, this month's flavor, was out of the question. He tried to refocus. What about Claire? There was a good woman. She was hard working, feminine, beautiful, and the life of the party, but. . .what was it that was missing? He stared into the fire as though it held the answers.

"What's so interesting in that fire?" His mother's voice was warm and teasing. "Got something on your mind?" There was no fooling his mother.

"Just thinking." He smiled up at her as she leaned down, one arm circling his shoulders, just like the night he found out about the real Jennifer.

"You're thinking awfully hard."

"You don't give up, do you?"

"Not when it comes to you. If I acquiesced every time you

said you didn't want to talk, I'd never know what was going on with you. It's like pulling teeth to get anything out of you." She rumpled his hair. He chuckled, a smile tugging at the corners of his mouth.

"You're probably right."

"No probably about it. I'm your mother. I'm always right."

"Okay, okay. I give up." He held his hands up in surrender. "What do you want to know?"

"What's bothering you." It was a statement not a question. He thought about it a while.

"I was just thinking how hard it is to find a good woman these days."

"There are still a few out there. Don't give up." She patted him on the shoulder. "God will let you know when it's the right one. He'll bring her to you when it's time."

"What if she's here and I'm overlooking her because I'm so picky?"

"God won't let you overlook her, and being picky is not a bad thing. You deserve the best, and I'm not saying that just because I'm your mother. God wants the best for all his children."

"I guess you're right." A sense of peace settled over him. He rose from his chair and hugged her. "You're a real sharp cookie, you know that?"

"It's about time someone noticed." They both laughed. "Let's join your father. He's starting to look lonely."

"Where is Alex anyway?" Scott glanced around the room.

"On the phone. Where else?"

&

"Look, Carly, I told you not to call anymore. It's over." Alex hung up the phone with a little more force than was necessary. His patience was wearing thin, and he was an extremely patient man. He heard the sound of his mother's voice and caught the end of their conversation. Remaining in the shadows, he waited till they went into the living room. It reminded him of another time when standing in the shadows he had heard his parent's talking:

"I just don't know what to do with Alex. He's driving me crazy. Why can't he be more like Scott? Scott never gives us any trouble."

"I don't know, dear. I just don't know."

From that moment on he had known that Scott was the favorite. No matter what he did, he couldn't measure up to Scott. If Alex received high honors, Scott would get even higher honors. Whatever he did, Scott did it better. Eventually, he decided that being a rebel was the only thing he was better at than Scott. Being bad was his trademark, something of his very own. Now he had one more thing on Scott, and it was time for the unveiling. He moved toward the living room, his victory smile in place.

❧

"There you are, Alex. We were wondering where you had gotten off to," his mother said. The smile didn't escape her notice. "What's up?"

"Why do you ask?" he asked, raising his eyebrows.

"You just look like you received good news."

"Oh, you mean the phone call. No, that was a bit of unpleasantness, but that's all over with now." He settled into the chair like a cat who had just eaten a bowl of cream. He sat with his hands folded on his stomach, watching his father twitch with curiosity.

"Are you going to let us in on your little secret?" his father asked gruffly. Alex enjoyed baiting his father. Patience was the one virtue Alex had acquired over the years, and he knew how to use it to his advantage.

"Maybe. Then again I don't want to speak too soon."

"For heaven's sake, Alex, quit talking in circles." His father hit the arm of his chair in frustration. "Either say something or be quiet."

"Now, dear, there's no need to get upset." There she went again, calming father down. How many times had she done that. These were the only times he felt his mother's love. "Alex, is there something you want to tell us?" She gave him the "I've had enough" look.

"Well, it may be premature, but. . ." he paused for effect, "I may be going on a trip soon."

"A trip? Where?" His mother looked puzzled.

"Down the aisle." He watched in silent satisfaction as his words registered. His father and mother looked stunned, but Alex concentrated on Scott. "Well, Golden Boy, what do you think?"

"You're getting married?" Scott couldn't believe his ears. He must have misunderstood.

"That's what I just said. Are you feeling well, little brother?" Alex tried to keep the sarcasm out of his voice as he noted the red creeping up Scott's neck.

"Who?"

"Elizabeth Jordan." Alex waited for Scott's reaction, savoring the moment.

"The Elizabeth Jordan that works at the firm?" his father asked.

"That's the one."

"But I thought. . ." She stopped in mid-sentence. Alex knew the rest, but he only smiled at her confusion. She glanced over at Scott whose face had gone from red to a pale shade of gray. "When did all this happen?"

"We've been going out for a couple of months now."

"A couple of months? Alex, do you really know this girl? Are you sure?" His mother's forehead wrinkled in concern.

"Yes, mother. I'm sure. I told her how I felt, and we decided she should take the holidays to think it over. Though I don't foresee any problems."

"So, she hasn't said yes?" Scott finally managed to get out.

"Not exactly, but I'm sure she will." Alex leaned back in his chair, the essence of calm assurance.

"Well, I. . .that's wonderful, dear. We're very happy for you." She said the words, but Alex could tell her heart wasn't in it. She was feeling sorry for Scott. . . He could see it in her eyes. "Isn't that right, dear?" She nudged her husband, and he mumbled an incoherent agreement. Nothing ever suited him.

"Congratulations, Alex," Scott managed. Alex saw him almost choke on the words. Triumph at long last.

"Thanks, Golden Boy. Well, I hate to eat and run, but I don't want to miss Elizabeth's call." He stood and grabbed his coat from the back of the chair.

"Of course not, dear. Let us know when you hear something more." She walked him to the door.

"I don't feel right about this. Something's wrong," the elder McClintock muttered. "I don't like it, not at all."

ঽ

Scott made his excuses and headed toward home. His heart was still in his stomach where it had dropped after Alex's announcement. Marriage? Alex was going to marry Elizabeth? His dinner turned to stone at the thought. He had imagined that Elizabeth was just another fling, but now she would be his sister-in-law. The thought hit him like a sledgehammer. Why was he so upset anyway? She wasn't the kind of girl he wanted. Let Alex have her. Maybe it would straighten Alex out.

Back home, Scott opened the medicine cabinet, looking for some cure for the tightness in his chest or the rock in his stomach. He chalked it up to indigestion, but in his heart he knew that there was no cure for what ailed him.

sixteen

Elizabeth stumbled into her apartment, dumping mail all over the floor. She dropped the suitcases, closing and locking the door behind her, before stooping to gather the scattered mail. You'd think she'd been gone a month, instead of just a week. She flipped through the mail. Nothing urgent. She put it on the desk in the hallway and lugged her suitcase into the bedroom. There was nothing worse than unpacking. Staring at the suitcase, hands on hips, she decided that it could wait until tomorrow. Tomorrow. The thought sent her heart skipping. Tomorrow she would tell Alex her decision. She took a deep breath and looked in the mirror. What was her problem? The other girl refused to answer. She changed into a pair of loose sweats, grabbed a cup of hot tea and settled with her mail on the couch. She would be like Scarlett O'Hara—she wouldn't think about it today.

❧

Alex arrived promptly at nine-thirty. Elizabeth looked ready on the outside, but inside she was a mess. Her heart beat double-time as she caught sight of him through the peephole. *Steady girl, steady.* She breathed a deep sigh and opened the door.

"Hi, Alex."

"Hi, Alex. Is that all I get after a week away?" He stepped over the threshold and closed the door in one fluid move. Sweeping her into his arms, he held her tight and lowered his lips to hers. Moments later, she finally caught her breath.

"I guess I don't have to ask if you missed me?" He chuckled and buried his face in her hair.

"Of course I missed you." She cleared her throat and started to speak, but he held up a hand in protest. "Don't say anything. When I propose officially, I want to do it right, so hold that thought—I hope it's a good thought." He smiled down at her, but the smile wavered at the corners.

"If you say so." She enjoyed the fact that he was afraid she would say no. It gave her confidence. She took delight in ignoring his last comment all together. Looking at her watch, she said, "We'd better hurry or we'll be late."

"All right. Let's go." He helped her into her coat and down the stairs. His hand encircling hers in a tight grip. It felt nice. It felt right.

❧

Sunday went by like any other normal Sunday, but Elizabeth couldn't shake her nervousness. He dropped her off after dinner with a quick kiss on the cheek. True to his word, he didn't mention anything about "the question."

Monday, she found a mound of papers that looked more like a mountain. She was just sorting through the stack when Alex popped in looking a bit ruffled.

"Alex, what're you doing down here so early in the morning?"

"Unfortunately, it's to bring bad news." His grim expression caused her heart to race.

"What's wrong?" Her alarmed tone brought a sudden softening to his face. He pulled her close, gently pushing the hair away from her face.

"I didn't mean to upset you. I just found out that I have to go out of town for a couple of days. It's just business."

She released the breath that had threatened to choke her only minutes ago. "Oh. I thought someone had died or something." He laughed, releasing the tension.

"No. Nothing like that." He paused and let his hand trace the curve of her chin. Her heart skipped, and she fought a sudden urge to run. "I just hate to leave you again so soon. Especially now."

"Oh." It was all she could think to say. She felt her nerves on edge and could feel her knees trembling. Was this the way love was supposed to feel? Of course it was, she chided herself. She was just nervous because it was her first real relationship.

Everybody got scared.

"Hey. What are you thinking so hard about?"

She jerked back to the reality of Alex's arms. "I'll miss you."

"Good. For a minute there I was afraid. . .well, never mind. I'll only be gone a few days." He touched her hair one more time. "I've got to go pack. I'll call you later in the week." He leaned down and kissed her softly on the lips and then disappeared down the hall.

As soon as she saw him turn the corner, she closed the door and sank into her chair. Her knees were still trembling and her pulse was uneven. What a relief! Why was she relieved that he was gone? She was supposed to be in love. It was just the tension getting to her. It was just nerves. *All women get nervous when a man proposes, right? Right.* She pushed the thoughts aside and buried herself in her work.

❧

Alex moved silently down the hall like a panther stalking his prey. He entered the apartment building the essence of calm, but inside a river of rage was welling up. She had gone too far! The ringing of the doorbell signaled the beginning of round one.

"Alex, what a nice surprise!" Carly held the door open for him to enter.

"Cut the niceties, Carly! What do you want?" Each word was ground out until it sounded more like a command than a question.

"I just want what's coming to me."

"Exactly what do you think you have coming to you?"

"A little respect."

"Respect?" Alex's laugh was harsh.

"Don't laugh at me!" Carly's voice raised to that whine he found so annoying.

"What do you really want?" At his tone, she straightened up and threw off pretense.

"I suggest that you take a different tone of voice or your pretty little fiance might get a phone call telling her exactly what kind of business trip you were really on." His eyebrows raised. "You didn't think I knew about her, did you? What, do you think I'm stupid?"

"I guess I underestimated you, but don't make the same mistake." Then he grabbed her throat and held her face inches from his own. "Because if I ever hear from you again I won't be responsible for my actions."

He let her go, and she fell back on a chair, holding her throat. He threw a stack of bills on the table, straightened his tie, and walked out, closing the door quietly behind him.

&

Carly gathered the money together. Her face began to burn. What had happened to her? She looked at the bills in her hands and something inside her broke. Hot tears washed down her cheeks and a sob formed in her throat. She suddenly felt the need for a shower, but no matter how she scrubbed she couldn't wash away the memories. Stumbling from the bathroom, she collapsed on her bed in sobs. "Oh, God, what have I become?"

seventeen

Alex called Elizabeth on Friday morning to say he would pick her up Saturday at six. She hung up the phone with a mixture of excitement and nervousness. Her week had been peaceful and busy, filled with catching up on work left from the holidays and going out with the girls. It had been a long time since she had spent time with other women. Alex had taken up all her time and effort. What was she saying? If other people could hear her thoughts they would think Alex was a job or a hobby, not the man she was in love with. *Are you really in love?* The little voice deep inside echoed in her mind. She silenced it by calling Morgan to make lunch plans.

The rest of the day was filled with last-minute reports and cleanup. Then she was free for the weekend. She drug herself up the stairs to her townhouse and collapsed on the couch. She would have stayed there, but the growling of her stomach sent her in search of food. The cabinets were almost bare because she hadn't been shopping since before the holidays. She groaned as she checked each cabinet and the refrigerator twice. A flier that was hanging on the refrigerator door by a small angel magnet caught her eye. It proclaimed "The best Chinese restaurant in town." The magnet said, "You are what you eat." She decided with a grin that she would be Chinese tonight. Squinting her eyes, she did an imitation of a geisha girl and then remembered that was Japanese. She had to get a grip on herself.

It was only a few blocks to the restaurant, so Elizabeth pulled her coat close around her chin and walked briskly. Looking up, she could just make out a few stars in the night sky. The rest were lost in the blaze of lights across the horizon. She sighed as she thought of the open skies of the country, and nights sitting on the patio staring at the unending sky. Tonight it felt good to be alone. The brisk air invigorated Elizabeth, and she soon found herself humming a song. The humming stopped abruptly when she saw who was coming out of the restaurant directly in front of her. Her heart began to pound and her face began to burn. She looked around for a place to hide, but it was too late. He had seen her, and they were coming her way.

"Hello, Elizabeth."

"Hello, Scott and Claire, isn't it?"

"Yes. It's nice to see you again." Claire smiled, oblivious to the tension.

"I hear congratulations might be in order." Scott smiled, but it didn't reach his eyes. "You seemed to have done the impossible."

"And what is that?" she asked, unreasonably irritated by his tone.

"Taming my brother."

"I didn't do anything."

"You give yourself too little credit, but I don't want to keep you from your dinner. I'm sure Alex will be here soon, and I need to get Claire in out of the cold." He nodded good-bye and tucked Claire's hand into the crook of his arm. Claire threw a good-bye over her shoulder, and then they were gone, leaving a breath of cold air from the open door. Elizabeth shivered, staring out into the night.

"Table for one." Elizabeth jumped.

"Yes." She followed the waiter through a maze of tables and sank gratefully into the booth. Her legs were suddenly weak and her appetite had disappeared. She hoped she wasn't catching the flu. She ordered Egg Drop Soup, an eggroll, and fried rice. And when the food arrived had to force herself to swallow each bite.

The walk home was less than enjoyable. Sudden clouds had obscured the stars, and a bitter wind blew through the layers of her coat, all the way to her skin. By the time she reached the townhouse, she only wanted a hot bath and to go to bed. As she fell asleep, she saw Scott holding Claire's hand, but then the image blurred and the hand was hers.

a

Elizabeth awoke dreading the day ahead. She spent the day restless and bored. Nothing could hold her attention. She looked at her Bible on the nightstand, but didn't pick it up. That was where she had always gone for solace before, but today she rebelled against the thought. At three o'clock, she began preparations for the night ahead. She had this same feeling the night of the prom in high school, a mixture of excitement, nausea, and fear. She chose a red dress that was fitted to the waist and then flared in soft folds to her ankles. It was Alex's favorite color. He always complimented her when she wore red. She turned in front of the mirror and was pleased by the way it flattered her figure. She spent extra time on her makeup, trying to get just the right shade of lipstick. Despite her early start, she was still fussing in front of the mirror when the doorbell rang.

She looked through the peephole and then took a deep breath, willing herself to calm down. Then, with trembling fingers, she unlocked and opened the door.

"Hi." The sight of him in a dark suit almost took her breath away. It looked like it was made especially for him. Knowing Alex that was extremely possible.

"Hi." He looked her over from head to toe, and she blushed under his scrutiny. "You look gorgeous. My lady in red." His smile of approval sent her spirits soaring.

"You don't look so bad yourself." She tried to sound sophisticated, but her voice sounded shaky at best.

"Maybe we should start a mutual admiration society. Let's go and see if we can get any more members for our fan club." He held out her coat.

"Where are we going anyway?" She asked as she buttoned up.

"That's a surprise." He pulled the door open and followed her out to the car. He put his hand under her elbow to help her down the stairs and held the car door open until she was settled. She revelled in the attention.

He drove to their favorite restaurant in Little Italy. The normally crowded restaurant seemed unnaturally quiet. *Had they gone out of business?* Her spirits dropped at the thought. But Alex didn't seem to notice anything unusual. He got out of the car and came around to open her door.

"Let's go, gorgeous. It's cold out here." He held his hand out to help her out of the car.

"Are you sure they're open?" Her brows furrowed in uncertainty.

"It's Saturday night. They're always open on Saturday night." He tugged her arm and she followed. Expecting the door to be locked, she was surprised when the door opened easily. "Ladies first." He ushered her inside.

"Ms. Jordan and Mr. McCLintock. It's so good to see you again. Would you like your usual table?" Mario's voice held no hint of any trouble. Elizabeth couldn't help wondering what had happened. Then as Mario turned to show them to their table Elizabeth gasped. The whole restaurant had been cleared and their favorite booth had been moved to the middle of the room. The table was covered in white linen and a dozen red roses in a crystal vase adorned the center of the table. It was set with real silver and china. The whole room was filled with flowers and the only lighting came from candles scattered about the room. The booth faced the picture window which looked out on the harbor. Elizabeth turned to Alex, her eyes wide in suprise.

"Do you like it?" he asked, tilting his head toward the room.

"Like it? It's. . .it's. . ."

"It's what?" he asked, amused by her sudden lack of speech.

"It's wonderful." She gazed around the room once more. "How did you do it?"

"That's my secret." He held out his arm. "Shall we go in or would you rather stand here and look at it all night?"

She put her hand in the crook of his arm and entered the fairyland. She was pampered all evening. Food was brought without a word. When a wine bottle was brought out, Elizabeth felt a moment of indecision, but Alex quickly allayed her fears. He pointed to the label which read sparkling white grape juice. "It looks just like champagne." She was delighted.

The evening went by like a storybook romance. Alex spent the whole night telling her how wonderful she was and how beautiful she looked. The waiters slipped in and out like ghosts. After the first course had been served, a string quartet appeared and began playing softly. Elizabeth began to wonder if it was all a dream, but it was real, and it was happening to her.

When the last of the dishes had been taken away, Alex reached into his pocket and pulled out two velvet boxes. She held her breath and her pulse began to race, as he took her hand in his.

"Elizabeth. A few weeks ago I told you that I loved you and I wanted you to be in my life. I meant every word of it. Elizabeth, would you do me the honor of becoming my wife?" Alex opened the smaller box and pulled out the largest diamond solitaire that she had ever seen. It sparkled in the candlelight. She nodded, unable to speak the words. He slipped the ring onto her finger and she turned it to catch the light. He kissed her hand and then pulled her close to him and kissed her on the lips. "You've made me a very happy man." Alex picked up the larger box and gave it to her.

"What's this?"

"Why don't you open it and find out?" He leaned back and smiled, relaxed now that the hard part was over.

She pulled back the cover, revealing a diamond pendant and matching earrings. She gasped. He took the necklace from its case and put it around her neck.

"They're a set. I thought we should keep the family together."

Elizabeth fingered the necklace unable to speak. Alex pulled her close and whispered in her ear. "Let's go home." She closed the box with the earrings and gathered up her coat. Alex held her hand all the way home. They were both silent, unwilling to break the spell.

At the townhouse, Alex took her keys and opened the door. He didn't wait to be invited. He walked in and put his coat on the back of a chair. She followed suit. He put in a Nat King Cole CD and pulled her into his arms. They danced slowly, circling the tiny space. He whispered her name and traced her face with the back of his knuckles. Then he kissed her neck softly, his arms pulling her closer. He kissed her deeper and deeper and she felt caught up in the warmth of the feeling. The music sounded far away. Elizabeth opened her eyes to find they had danced into the bedroom. Alex's hand on the zipper of her dress brought her back to reality with a jerk.

"No, Alex," she whispered, grabbing his hand.

"Come on, Elizabeth." He coaxed kissing lightly along her neck.

"No. It's not right."

"Sure it is. We're going to be married soon. It couldn't be more right." He continued to stroke her back. She grabbed both of his hands and pushed away from him.

"Alex, I want to wait until my wedding night. I want it to be special."

"It will be special." He tried to pull her back.

"Please, Alex. I want to wait."

He pulled away, the anger obvious in his eyes, but he sounded calm. "Whatever you want, Elizabeth, but I can't stay here any longer. I'll see you in the morning." He grabbed his coat as he moved toward the door. He was gone before she could say anything.

Elizabeth got ready for bed, but she could still feel the warmth of his body and then a new warmth flooded her face as she realized how close she had come. So many times she had ridiculed people for giving in to temptation, and here she had almost done the same thing. She knew that she was just as guilty of sin as the people she had judged, but instead of turning to God, she cried tears of shame into her pillow. The glitter of the diamond on her finger had turned to cold hard stone.

eighteen

Sunday morning, Alex was his usual self. He made no mention of the night before, and Elizabeth silently breathed a prayer of thanks. She wanted to forget the whole thing. Well not the whole thing, just the last part. She forced herself to think about Alex's proposal and the beautiful, romantic evening. A smile appeared on her face at the memory of the candlelit room. Fingering the diamond on her finger, she slipped her hand into the crook of his arm. He looked over at her and smiled, causing her heart to flutter at the mere look of him. She basked in the companionable silence of the car. It was nice knowing that they could just enjoy each other's presence. She leaned her head on his shoulder with a sigh.

"What are you thinking about?" His smile broadened and he looked down at her as if he knew the answer already.

"Last night. Our future. Everything." She let out a contented sigh.

"Is that all?" he drawled.

"Is there anything else?" she replied, looking up at him through her lashes.

"How about how beautiful you look?" He rubbed his cheek against the top of her hair. "Or, how we are going to tell my parents?" She sat upright. "Don't look so alarmed. They're only my family, not a bunch of headhunters."

His last words didn't register because her mind was suddenly filled with an image of Scott. She was going to marry Scott's brother. How in the world was she going to face him? He obviously didn't think too highly of her. What would Alex's parents think of her? Alarms went off in her head erasing the fairytale "happily ever after" atmosphere she had created. Alex was speaking, she tried to focus on his voice.

"Sweetheart, are you all right?" She realized Alex had asked her something.

"I'm sorry. What did you say?" she asked sheepishly.

"I said you don't have to worry. They're not a bunch of ogres." He smiled down at her and patted her arm.

"Do you think. . .do you think. . .they'll like me?"

"Like you? Of course they'll like you. They're going to love you. Father has always admired your work, and once they get to know you better they will adore you as much as I do. Now stop worrying your pretty little head about it. Everything will be just fine."

Elizabeth nodded her head in agreement, but her eyes belied her true feelings. They were clouded with doubt and a flicker of resentment at his patronizing tone. What was she thinking? Alex was just trying to make her feel better. She swallowed back the resentment and leaned back against his shoulder.

"That's better." He patted her hand. "Now, we'll just pop over for dinner tonight and it will be all over."

"Tonight!" She sat upright again. This time she turned in her seat and looked at him.

"Now don't get upset. There's nothing to worry about. I told them I had someone I wanted them to meet. We might as well share the good news while we're there."

The blood pounded in her ears, half out of nervousness and half out of anger. "How could you make plans without telling me?"

"I am telling you." His face was implacable, and her anger mounted.

"I meant before you made plans."

"I thought you would want to meet the family and share the good news as soon as possible."

She breathed in deeply and tried to control her temper. It was just because she was nervous. There was no need to get angry. He was only excited to share the good news with his family.

"When are we supposed to be there?" Her voice was back

to normal, but her attitude was still tense.

"About six. That way we can chat a little while before dinner."

She might have said more, but at that moment they pulled into the church parking lot. Maybe the less said the better. There was no sense getting into an argument over it. He came around and helped her out of the car. She took his arm and fixed a smile on her face, but her back was stiffer than a pew as they walked to the double oak doors.

Elizabeth hardly noticed the sermon or the hymns they sang. Her mind was filled with dread at the coming meeting. Would Scott be there? She hoped not. She couldn't stand the thought of dealing with his obvious dislike through what would already be a grueling experience. She tried to shake the thoughts away. Alex's parents were bound to be nice. She shouldn't think about it like this. She was just going to drive herself crazy.

The ending prayer couldn't have come soon enough for Elizabeth. She pulled Alex toward the double doors, but he didn't budge. He took her left hand and began showing off the ring to his friends. Murmured congratulations and little gasps of awe followed one right after the other as he displayed her to every passerby. She whispered forced thank-you's and smiled, while on the inside she twitched with impatience. All she wanted to do was to get away. Finally, the last of the well-wishers left, and Alex walked her to the front doors. His arm, which had been draped possessively around her shoulders through the whole ordeal, suddenly dropped to his side. Once inside the car she let her feelings be known.

"Why did you do that?"

"Do what?" he asked innocently.

"Show me off like I was some kind of prize you had won." Her hands were balled into fists in her lap.

"Sweetheart, I'm just proud that you're mine." The words should have made her happy, but for some reason she felt angry.

"I felt like I was on display."

"I just wanted everyone to share in our happiness. I'm sorry if I made you uncomfortable. I'll be more sensitive next time." He gave her that sad-puppy look, and she felt her anger lessening. "Forgive me?"

"I suppose." He gave her one of his heart-stopping smiles and she melted. She felt her face relaxing into a smile.

"That's better. Now come here." He pulled her close and kissed her hungrily. "I've been thinking about that all morning." He ran his forefinger over her face.

"You were supposed to be thinking about the sermon." She tried to look stern, but couldn't hide the smile that tugged at the corners of her mouth.

"Who can think about a sermon when you're sitting next to me?" She could feel the tension between them and knew he wanted more than just a kiss. She leaned back in her seat.

"Who's going to be at dinner tonight?" Her question broke the connection, and he turned to start the engine.

"Just Mother and Father."

"Do you always call them that?" she asked, suddenly curious.

"That's what they are: my mother and father." He looked straight ahead.

"Don't you ever call them Mom or Dad," she questioned.

"No." His mood changed as quickly as the sun setting and no attempts by Elizabeth could draw him back into conversation. She finally lapsed into silence and looked out the window for the remainder of the trip.

Once in the restaurant, Alex returned to his charming self. Elizabeth was beginning to wonder which was his true self. The charming man beside her who had swept her off her feet or the silent and withdrawn man in the car. They spent lunch chatting about nothing in particular, trying to stay away from anything serious.

That afternoon, Alex took her to an art exhibit across town. She followed him around the room feeling decidedly out of place. The art that adorned the walls looked like meaningless globs of paint to her. Alex, on the other hand, chatted knowledgeably with the artists and other guests. She smiled and held on to Alex's arm, nodding in agreement when necessary.

Finally, at five, they left the gallery. Elizabeth sighed in relief. Alex must have caught her mood for he commented, "Didn't you enjoy the exhibit?"

"It was okay." She tried to sound convincing. He smiled at her failed attempt.

"It'll grow on you. Next time we'll go when it's quieter and I'll teach you all you need to know about modern art." She tried not to scowl in distaste at the mention of returning, only nodding in agreement. He held the car door for her. "Now, off to the parents."

With each mile, she grew more nervous. Alex chatted easily about art, the family home, his childhood. Anything to keep her mind occupied, but she wasn't listening. The only thing she could hear was the pounding of her heart.

They arrived promptly at six. The house was Victorian, complete with gables and a wrap-around porch with a swing. Elizabeth had dreamed of living in a house like this. A wild rabbit hopped into the shrubs, and she wished she could stay out here in the peaceful twilight, but Alex propelled her toward the door. A lovely woman in her fifties greeted them at the door. She had silver hair and dark blue eyes that contrasted with her son's dark good looks.

"Hello. You must be Elizabeth." She ushered Elizabeth in and enfolded her in a gentle hug. "Alex has told us a lot about you." Elizabeth relaxed as she felt the welcome in his mother's touch and smiled in return.

"I'm glad to finally meet you, Mrs. McClintock."

"No need for all the formalities. My name is Katherine."

"Thank you, . . .Katherine." Elizabeth felt strange calling Alex's mother by her first name, but the feeling soon faded in the warmth of the woman's personality.

"Matthew, come here and meet Elizabeth," Katherine called. Mr. McClintock came into the foyer and his presence seemed to fill every nook and cranny.

"We've already met, dear. She works for me, remember?" Matthew McClintock answered. He shook Elizabeth's hand and motioned her toward the living room. Elizabeth noticed that father and son did not embrace, but merely inclined their heads in acknowledgment.

"In that case, you won't mind if I steal her away to the kitchen for a little girl talk." Her husband chuckled and waved them toward the kitchen. Elizabeth was stunned at the way a smile transformed his face from cold-hearted businessman to tender grandfather. She followed Katherine into a large kitchen decorated in antique white and country blue. All the appliances were white, including the old one-armed refrigerator.

"I haven't seen one of those in ages." Elizabeth pointed to the refrigerator. "Wherever did you find it?"

"It belonged to my mother. It's old as the hills and breaks down about every other month it seems. Matt keeps urging me to buy a new one with an icemaker, but I love this old thing. It's one of the few things I have left of my mother's. That and my china."

"I love old things." Elizabeth wandered around the kitchen lovingly touching the old cabinets. Katherine checked the roast in the oven and then leaned back against the sink.

"I guess I don't have to ask how you two met."

"No. That's obvious."

"What brought you two together? You're not the type of girl Alex usually goes out with." Katherine held up her hands in defense. "I'm not saying that's bad. It's just he usually goes for looks and not depth. Not that you're not pretty. Oh my, I am getting myself in a fix." Katherine's cheeks flushed as she groped about for a way out of the situation.

"It's okay. I know what you mean. I was surprised when Alex asked me out."

"Dear me, I didn't mean to say that you aren't attractive."

"I know you didn't." Elizabeth crossed the space between them and patted Katherine on the arm. "He asked me out for lunch one day. We went out and he kept coming back."

"I can see why." Katherine squeezed her arm and smiled. "Why don't we take dinner in before those two get too engrossed in business talk?"

Together they brought the food to the dining room and Elizabeth felt at home. It had been a long time since she had helped her mother set the table. It was nice to be part of a family that she could call her own. She put down the last dish just as Katherine called the men in for dinner.

"Let's join hands and pray." Elizabeth looked up in surprise at Mr. McClintock. She could not get used to thinking of him as anything other than the boss. She squeezed Alex's hand in delight as his father blessed the food. Alex returned the pressure. Dinner conversation consisted mostly of small talk about the firm, the weather, how they had met. After they had finished the main course, Katherine returned with plates of apple pie and a pot of coffee. As soon as his mother had finished serving everyone, Alex cleared his throat and tapped his water glass with his spoon. The clink brought silence, and Elizabeth's heart seemed loud to her ears. Though, no one else seemed to notice.

"I have an announcement."

"Yes, dear." His mother looked at him expectantly.

"Last night I asked Elizabeth to marry me and she said yes." Alex smiled and waited for their reaction.

"That's wonderful, darling." His mother was the first to respond. She obviously approved of his choice. His father was a little slower in reacting, but seemed happy.

"Well, I never thought I would see the day when a woman could tame my son. You must be quite a lady." He held his water glass in salute.

"That she is, Father." Alex raised his glass in return. The ladies joined them, and they toasted their marriage. Dessert and coffee were blended with congratulations and questions about the future.

"Have you thought about a date?" his father asked.

Elizabeth was opening her mouth to answer no, when Alex

said, "We were thinking about the first of the year." Elizabeth hid her surprise and her rising anger.

"Do you think that's enough time, Alex?" His mother looked skeptical.

"Of course it is, Mother. I've been looking for Elizabeth all my life, and I don't want to waste another moment." Alex looked at Elizabeth across the table. She swallowed her anger, fear replacing it as she counted the days. "Speaking of time, I think we'd better head back."

Elizabeth went through the formalities of thanking his parents and saying good-bye, but her mind was on Alex's announcement. She waited until Alex turned onto the main road before she spoke.

"Why did you say we had discussed the first of the year? We haven't even talked about a date, yet."

"We didn't? I was sure we had, darling." He stroked her hair, but she pulled away.

"You know we didn't."

"I guess I got ahead of myself a little."

"A little!" Alex pulled off the main road onto what could barely be called a track and turned off the car and the lights. He reached across the car and pulled her into his arms. Before she had time to think, he was kissing her. His lips held hers until she gasped for a breath.

"I want you so much, Elizabeth." His voice was husky and his eyes were filled with a look that frightened her. "You want to wait until we get married. Fine, but I can't wait much longer." He kissed her tenderly and then released her, putting his hands back on the wheel. "Do you understand?"

She nodded, but said nothing. He started the engine and they drove home in silence. Something in the way he had looked at her sent a shiver of fear along her spine. She tried to imagine herself married to Alex in five weeks, but she couldn't comprehend what that would be like. Did she really know this man? The silence was heavy as each pondered their own thoughts. Alex gave her a quick kiss on the cheek and then hurried off without even walking her to the door. She stood on the sidewalk watching until his brake-lights disappeared. A cold wind sent her for the warmth of her townhouse, but even the comfort of home couldn't dispel her fears

nineteen

Elizabeth didn't have much time to think about her fears. She was soon immersed in a flood of activity. Alex was planning a huge engagement party for the following week, to be held at his house, with Elizabeth as the hostess. Engagement parties weren't usually given by the couple, she had argued, but Alex brushed her off, saying he liked to be different from the crowd. Elizabeth felt she was in over her head. She had never dealt with caterers or maids before, and to top it off Alex had invited fifty guests. Elizabeth had to take two days off of work to deal with all the arrangements. She mentioned to Alex that she was getting behind at work because of the party, and he had merely mentioned that she could quit once they were married. At the time, she had resented the remark, but if this was going to be the norm in their marriage, something would have to be done. Somehow she managed to get everything ready with the help of a brilliant and very helpful caterer, who even managed to find time to help her pick out the floral arrangements and organize the staff. Looking around, Saturday morning, she was proud of the way the house looked. She gave her approval and left the rest in Judith's capable hands as she went home to get ready.

She hadn't even had time to think what she would wear to this affair. Maybe Judith could help. She hesitated to call on her again for advice. She mentally walked through her closet as she drove home and pulled into her driveway. She was so lost in her thoughts that she almost knocked over a delivery man as she walked up the path. She stopped short of bumping into him.

"Excuse me." She stepped back to avoid stepping on his heels.

"Quite all right, madame." His words sounded humble, but

were delivered in a tone that was almost arrogant.

"Can I help you?" she asked as he turned to go up her walk.

"I'm to deliver this to Miss Elizabeth Jordan." He held a dress bag draped carefully over his arm.

"I'm Elizabeth Jordan." She reached for the bag, but he pulled back.

"I'll carry it, Miss." She pulled her hand back as if stung and preceded him to the door. She unlocked the door and stepped inside. The little man carried the dress inside and hung it on the coatrack in the corner. He gave a quick little bow and was gone.

Whatever could it be? she wondered. She didn't remember ordering anything. There was a card with her name on it pinned to the garment bag. It read: To my darling, love Alex. Unzipping the bag, Elizabeth gasped in admiration. She reached out to touch a black velvet evening gown which bore the name of a prominent designer. The diamond necklace that Alex had given her would complement the deep V-neck. It had a fitted bodice that flared gracefully to the floor. It looked just like a dress that Audrey Hepburn or Deborah Kerr would wear. In the back of the garment bag there was a pocket and Elizabeth discovered a matching pair of velvet pumps. Alex had thought of everything.

She carried the dress to her bedroom and hung it carefully on the closet door with the shoes underneath. She hummed a little tune as she started her bath, adding lilac salts to the water. Her frustration at the week's work vanished as the bathroom began to smell like a private garden. She sank into the hot water and felt her muscles relax. She spent extra time on her toilette, doing her nails and taking extra time with her hair. By five o'clock she was dressed and took a turn at the mirror. The black velvet bodice fitted like a glove and complemented her figure. Then at the hips it flared into a silky material that seemed to float to the ground. She had her hair up in a French twist with little curls around her face that softened the look. Last of all she put on the diamond necklace and earrings. It was perfect. She whirled around the room feeling like a princess.

Alex picked her up a little after five and his expression said it all. He looked her over from head to foot, and she felt a blush steal up to her cheeks.

"Will I do?"

"You will most definitely do." He took her hand and gazed at her again. "We'd better go or we may never make the party," he whispered in her ear. A shiver went up her spine and she hurried to grab her purse and wrap.

"Then I guess we'd better go."

"I guess so." His answer was rather vague as though his mind was on something else, and he seemed hesitant to go. Then he snapped back and held out his arm to her. "Shall we?" he said with a bow.

"Let's," she replied with a curtsy.

&

The guests began arriving at six o'clock sharp. Elizabeth stood by Alex's side, greeting guests until she thought she would go mad trying to remember everyone's name. The McClintock's arrived and Katherine gave her a sympathetic squeeze before heading off to make sure all was well in the kitchen. Matthew McClintock made a beeline for the living room where one of his best clients was talking to a prominent senator. Everything was going smoothly until the last guest arrived. Elizabeth caught her breath at the sight of Scott McClintock in a black tuxedo. He seemed at home in it, even though he had admitted to feeling more comfortable in jeans that day at his house. She didn't want to think about that day. He was escorting Claire who was flawless in a short red dress and high heels. She made Elizabeth suddenly doubt her own appearance.

"Hello, Golden Boy." Alex slapped his brother on the back.

"Hello, Alex. I think you've both met Claire."

"Yes, of course." Alex was playing the charming host. He pulled Elizabeth to his side. "Glad you two could make it.

Why don't you go on in and enjoy yourselves."

Scott nodded curtly at Elizabeth and then moved into the living room and disappeared in the crowd. The crowd had spread from the living room to the library and on into the ballroom where a string quartet had begun to play. Elizabeth made the rounds at Alex's side, but her confidence was now gone and she felt claustrophobic. There was a wonderful buffet set up in the dining room, but she couldn't force herself to try any of Judith's delicious food. A knot had begun to grow in her stomach, choking any desire to eat.

Every once in a while she would spot Scott talking or eating, but always with Claire. Her eyes seemed to search for him constantly. She noticed how his broad shoulders looked in the dinner jacket. She watched his hands holding a glass or gesturing to make his point. Alex's hand on her shoulder made her jump as though she had been caught robbing the cookie jar.

"Everything all right? You look a little pale." His voice sounded concerned.

"I guess I'm tired. It's been a long day." She gave him a wan smile and he massaged her shoulders.

"It won't be much longer and then we can finally be alone." His eyes held a hint of mischief. He leaned in close to her ear as he spoke and then pulled her to him in a brief embrace. Elizabeth looked over his shoulder and her eyes locked with Scott's across the room. He was staring at her—she could have sworn he was angry.

Moments later, Scott made his way toward the door, giving Alex a quick nod and then disappeared. Elizabeth stared at the door with a mixture of relief and regret. What was she doing? She was going to marry Alex. She would just have to make peace with Scott, although she had never really been sure what the problem was in the first place. She sighed, and Alex slipped his arm around her in a protective gesture. She leaned her head back on his shoulder, grateful for the support.

Two hours later, the last of the guests took their leave. It was another half hour before the caterers and extra help were gone. Elizabeth looked around at what had once been a spotless room. Now, glasses of wine and plates of half-eaten food and napkins were scattered over every flat surface. The flowers, which had begun to wilt in the heat of so many bodies, had dropped their petals and the countless parade of shoes had embedded them in the carpet. Cigarette smoke hung in the air, giving Elizabeth a headache.

"You look done in, darling." He pulled her into his arms holding her close. "Why don't you stay here tonight?" She started to pull away from him. He held her tighter. "I didn't mean it that way. You just look so tired."

"I think it would be better if I went home. Besides, I want my own bed tonight."

"You mean it would be safer," Alex whispered in her ear.

"That too."

He sighed and then reached to help her with her coat.

"You're probably right."

He dropped her off at the door with a tender kiss and a "sleep well." She kicked her shoes into a corner and shed the beautiful clothes. It was way past midnight and Cinderella was tired of the ball gown. She hung it carefully in the garment bag and did a quick toilette. She expected to be asleep before her head hit the pillow, but sleep was slow in coming. Images of the party filtered through her mind until one image blotted out all the others. Scott's eyes locked on hers. As she fell asleep, she could still feel his eyes on hers.

❧

Scott watched Elizabeth as she greeted the guests. Her eyes were lit up with excitement, and he couldn't help noticing how beautiful she looked tonight. He positioned himself in the corner where he could see her without other people noticing. He tried to concentrate on the conversation at hand, but found his mind and his eyes continually wandering toward Elizabeth. The evening was straining his nerves to the breaking point. All these people with their cigarette smoke and reeking of alcohol made him want to escape, find some fresh air, but he knew he couldn't leave, at least not yet.

Scott mingled with his father's business associates. He introduced Claire to everyone because she was always at his elbow. He sometimes forgot that she was there. She was like a ring—he knew she was there, but he don't think about her. He was beginning to tire of taking her to all these parties and functions. The construction project would soon be completed and she would go back to New York, and he could go back to the farm for some peace and quiet. It seemed like years since he had had an entire weekend to relax or work on the farm. He tightened his grip on the glass of cola until it threatened to crack under the pressure.

Scott glanced at his watch and decided that he had fulfilled his brotherly duty. Looking around the room, he spotted Claire ensconced in the corner with some of his mother's friends. He hadn't realized she had left his side. As he tried to catch her eye, his glance landed on Alex whispering into Elizabeth's ear. The intimacy of the act caused a knot to form in his stomach. As Alex's arms encircled her waist and pulled her close, anger welled up in Scott's heart. For an instant, Elizabeth's eyes locked with his over Alex's shoulder and their gaze seemed to be held by invisible bonds. The connection was broken the instant Alex released her. Then Scott crossed the room to Claire. He had had enough for one night. Taking their coats to the door, he motioned to Alex that he was leaving.

The cold air felt good after the stuffy, smoke-filled house. He dropped Claire off at the hotel and headed for home. But even the peace of home was disrupted by images of Elizabeth in his brother's arms. He knelt by his bed and prayed for guidance, pouring out his pain and confusion to God. He didn't understand the turmoil in his heart, but he knew he couldn't handle it alone. After several minutes in prayer, he felt God's peace steal over him and he crawled into bed. Sleep soon claimed him, but his last thoughts were of Elizabeth.

twenty

From the night of her engagement on, Elizabeth's life was a roller coaster. The engagement party was only the beginning. When they weren't attending a party in their honor, Alex was taking her to the ballet, the opera, or more art museums. It was as if he was showing off a new sportscar to all his friends. Part of Elizabeth swelled with pride, but the rest of her was in rebellion. If it didn't stop soon, she was going to have to have a talk with Alex. Three weeks after the engagement party, Alex and Elizabeth were having lunch at Mario's when he dropped the next bomb.

"I told Mother that we would spend the week of Christmas and New Year's at the house." He spoke the words between bites of fettucinni as though he were announcing the weather.

"The whole week?" Elizabeth's fork stopped halfway to her mouth and hung suspended.

"Of course. It's a family tradition. Scott and I always come home for the week. It's our 'family' time." He continued to eat while reading a fax he had picked up from the office.

"What about my family?"

"Darling, you told me that you didn't have any close relations." He continued to read as he spoke.

"I do have friends." Her cheeks began to flush with anger.

"Of course, darling," he murmured without looking up. She slapped the fax onto the table with the palm of her hand.

"Don't ignore me. I said I have friends that I would like to visit over Christmas and New Year's." He looked at her hand and then slowly panned to her eyes.

"I wasn't ignoring you."

"Yes, you were. You had your head stuck in that fax."

"I heard every word that you said." His voice was calm and even, but she could sense that he was irritated by her action. "Maybe we should talk about this when one of us isn't being childish." He raised his hand and called for the check. "I'll get you a taxi back to the office. I have some errands to run."

All the way back, she seethed. The nerve of him! Who did he think he was? God? She replayed the scene over and over in her mind, getting angrier with every passing second. She fairly stomped back to her office and closed the door with a loud bang.

By the end of the afternoon, Elizabeth had cooled down somewhat. She realized that Alex was just used to getting his own way, and getting angry wouldn't solve anything. She would have to approach him in a calm and reasonable manner. The chance never came, though, because Alex sent word by his secretary that he would be out of town for the next two days and that he would be there in time for the anuual office Christmas party. He wanted her to be packed and ready to go to his parent's house that night.

Her face was set in a grim line as she cleaned up to go home. He had made sure that there would be no time for her to argue about it. He hadn't even left a number where he could be reached. She argued with the air all the way home, slapping the steering wheel for emphasis.

A good night's sleep calmed her and she began to rationalize the incident. He had probably been in such a rush that he hadn't had time to get a message to her and had thought the whole thing was settled. His mind had obviously been on business. She convinced herself that this was the truth and settled down to work.

That night she packed her bags, gathering together all the presents she had picked out for his family. There was an antique white vase that would look perfect in Katherine's kitchen and a gold tie clip with the image of a cross etched in the center. She had found both gifts in an antique store near the office. Scott's gift had been easy. She had been browsing in a used bookstore when she had come across a first-edition, leatherbound copy of Dwight L. Moody's sermons.

Instinctively she knew that he would enjoy it. Alex's gift, on the other hand, had been a nightmare. He bought whatever he wanted and she was unsure as to what he would prefer. She finally settled on a painting he had admired at one of the art exhibits. The price tag had made her cringe, but then again who was she to judge art?

She loaded the trunk with her treasures and fell into bed exhausted. She comforted herself that tomorrow was the last day of work before the holidays, but somehow that only made her more tired. She drifted off to sleep with visions of Scott holding his gift and smiling at her.

❧

The office was filled with Christmas cheer the next morning. The prospect of two weeks of vacation would make anyone happy. There were more smiles than usual as Elizabeth made her way down the hall. She found herself humming "Deck the Halls" as she typed out the last report of the year. There was great satisfaction in finishing the reports and filing away case files marked "closed." By mid-afternoon, her office was spotless. She locked the filing cabinets and her desk and looked around. A sudden feeling of dread washed over her; perhaps this would be her last day in this office. She shook it off, chalking it up to nervousness about the upcoming holidays and her upcoming marriage. Come the new year there would be lots of changes in her life. No wonder she was nervous.

She went down to the large conference room which had been transformed for the party tonight. Elizabeth and Morgan spent the afternoon decorating the tree and hanging tinsel and other decorations. The tree would only be seen tonight and then everybody would be gone for the holidays. It seemed a waste, but Alex insisted on it. The room soon looked like a winter fairyland with little white lights strung everywhere and the tree topped with fake snow. The smell of spiced apple cider began to fill the room as the caterers arrived and began to set up the buffet table. There was the traditional eggnog, as well as caviare and champagne. The elder McClintock did not approve, but made this one concession to his son. Soon the room began to buzz as groups began arriving from different parts of the office. At five o'clock, Elizabeth realized that Alex had not appeared yet.

True to form, he arrived fashionably late at five-fifteen. He searched the room until he spotted her behind the bowl of eggnog and then closed the space between them with a minimum of effort. He pulled her smoothly into the kitchenette and closed the door, capturing her mouth in a kiss before the door clicked shut.

"I missed you," he whispered, pulling her close to him. The embrace was so tight, Elizabeth felt trapped.

"I missed you to." Elizabeth pushed back to give herself some space.

"Then why are you pushing me away?" His eyes pierced into her.

"I'm just hot. I've been working all afternoon and this room is a little stuffy." She lied, but he accepted her excuse without comment. He relaxed his grip. "What have you been up to?"

"Just some follow-up work." The vagueness of his answer made Elizabeth feel vaguely uneasy. Before, he always included her in his work, telling her all about his cases. Maybe they were both feeling the strain of their parting. She decided that now was the time to sort out the matter of where she would spend Christmas and New Year's.

"Alex. I've been thinking about our last conversation." She hesitated, looking at his chest as she prepared her arguments. "I'm glad that we're going to your parents for the holidays. I really want to get to know them."

"That's good." His smile was that of a man who was confident that he had won the battle. He started to speak, but she interrupted him.

"But. . ." His smile faded. "But, I also want to go see my friends after Christmas. I thought we could go to their house for New Year's. My friends haven't even met you yet."

"I thought we had decided that we were spending the holidays with my parents." His lips were set in a line, a look she often saw on his face as he went into court.

"No. You announced that we were going to your parents. Then you left before we had time to discuss it."

"Family is more important than your friends."

"My friends are my family." Her eyes turned dark at his tone. "They were all I had when my parents died."

"Well, now you have us. We're your family now." His lips turned up in the corner, imitating a smile. But there was no warmth in his eyes. He put his arms out as if to comfort her, but she pushed away.

"They're still my friends." Her chin came up and she looked him squarely in the eye.

"Yes, of course they are, but since this is our first holiday together don't you think we should spend it with my family? You spent Thanksgiving with your friends. I'm sure they'll understand." His face returned to its normal position, knowing he had made a point she would be hard pressed to argue.

"I would still like to spend New Year's at Hope's." She remained firm despite his arguments and charming smile.

"Why don't we wait till later to talk about New Year's? Let's just enjoy tonight." He leaned down and kissed her cheek and then pulled her back into the party.

He was soon making the rounds. Elizabeth put on a smile, but inside she was still angry. She knew that no matter what he thought, she was going to Hope's house for New Year's.

Elizabeth told herself to forget it. She was not going to let it spoil her evening. She moved from group to group, catching up with friends. Soon, she was laughing and chatting. She caught Alex watching her from across the room. He smiled, but it was his victory smile from the courtroom. She smiled back because other people were watching, but it felt plastic on her face.

After the party, Alex insisted that she ride with him, but she argued that it wasn't safe to leave her car at the empty office building for two weeks. Alex finally agreed and they took separate cars. The silence was a relief to Elizabeth, and it allowed her to work out her thoughts and cool her temper.

She wondered if they were really suited for each other after all. Of course they were. All couples went through a period of adjustment. They would both have to learn to give and take. *Then why,* a voice whispered, *am I the one making all the adjustments?* The thought followed her all the way to the McClintock's house.

Alex helped her unload the presents and her bags and showed her into a room on the second floor. It was decorated in blue, her favorite color, and it had a bay window with a seat. She ran her hands across the cushions and looked out the window. She had always wanted a room like this with a window seat where she could curl up and read. She felt Alex's hand on her shoulder.

"A penny for your thoughts."

"I was just thinking how much I wanted a room like this when I was growing up."

"Then you shall have it. Whatever you want." He pulled her into his arms. And when she looked into his eyes, the look of the lawyer had been replaced by the look of a lover. He kissed her slowly and deeply and then released her with, "Good night, darling."

"Good night." All the fight seemed to leave her. Here was a man who wanted to give her everything. She felt ashamed that she had doubted him. Still, as she snuggled under the covers, the question still echoed in her mind: *Why am I the one making all the changes?* She pushed the thought away, replacing it with the image of his parting words and a dream of their new life together.

twenty-one

Elizabeth awoke to sunshine streaming through the bay window. It took her a moment to realize where she was. The McClintock's home. She fluffed the pillows and sat up to look around. Katherine's touch was evident in this room with its blue flowered wallpaper and pale blue carpet. The bed was covered with a white down quilt and trimmed in ruffles and lace. The curtains matched perfectly along with the accent cushions on the window seat. With two sons and no daughters, this room was probably Katherine's only chance to be totally feminine in her choice of decorations.

The wind howled in the trees and whipped around the house. Elizabeth snuggled underneath the covers. A glance at the clock told her it was time to get up, but her spirit rebelled. Just a few more minutes. She stretched like a cat woken from a long nap and then threw back the covers. Searching through her suitcase, she found a fleece suit of deep navy and white with socks and casual shoes to match. The guest room had its own bath decorated in the same colors with a seascape theme that was relaxing. As she soaked in the tub, she noted the pictures of lighthouses, shells, and colored pebbles placed carefully around the room. Katherine certainly had a knack for decorating. At that moment, Elizabeth felt the itch to decorate a home of her own. Ideas sprang into her mind of how each room would look. Her enthusiasm dissolved when she remembered that Alex's house was already decorated, and he certainly wouldn't want her changing his perfect house.

Finally the water cooled, and she got out of the tub. She looked at her image in the mirror as she brushed her dark hair. *What do I really want?* Still no answer from the girl in the mirror. She shrugged and pulled her hair back into a navy bow at the nape of her neck. Within minutes she was dressed and on her way.

As she went down the stairs, the scent of bacon and coffee greeted her. She followed the smell into the kitchen where Katherine was busy flipping an omelette. There was no trace of the men.

"There you are, dear. I was just about to go and call you for breakfast." Her future mother-in-law was dressed casually today in an outfit similar to her own.

"Where are the menfolk?"

"Out. Matthew had an appointment with a client in Washington, and Alex went along with him. He didn't want to wake you, so he told me to tell you to relax and enjoy yourself and that he would be back for dinner."

"Oh." Elizabeth felt her body relax. Somehow, with Alex gone, she felt free. Free from what she wasn't sure.

"Now, just sit down and relax. Breakfast will be ready in a minute. I hope you like omelettes."

"They're my favorite."

"Great."

Katherine served up breakfast, and they ate in quiet companionship. Then they made short work of the dishes and left the kitchen spotless. Katherine told her to make herself at home, while she ran some errands. Left alone in the house, Elizabeth began to explore.

Each of the rooms had its own theme, but all of them were done in either a blue, brown, gray, or ecru. The master bedroom was at the back of the house on the first floor with a connected master bath. The carpet was ecru, but was almost completely covered by an antique cherry bedroom suite. Besides the living room, dining room and kitchen, there was also a TV room with a pool table at one end. Upstairs there were two more bedrooms and another bathroom. The first room was obviously Alex's because his suitcases were laying on a chest at the end of the bed. It was the essence of neatness. Instead of posters of sports stars on the wall, Alex had honor awards and busts of Shakespeare and Beethoven as bookends. The next room was the guest room where she was staying. At the back, Elizabeth opened the last door. One whole wall was bookshelves filled to capacity. She saw almost the complete collection of "Hardy Boys" mysteries. Scattered around were trophies for different sports, mostly basketball. The bed was slightly rumpled as if the occupant had left in a hurry. There were stacks of annuals and magazines scattered across the floor. It looked as if he still lived there.

Curious, Elizabeth picked up an annual from the top of the stack. Flipping through the pages, she found pictures of Scott and Alex in high school. One picture caught her attention. Scott was surrounded by his parents as he received an award. Alex was standing next to them, but seemed separated somehow. But it was his expression that caught her attention. He was looking at Scott with contempt. Something about that picture made the hairs on the back of her neck stand at attention. She closed the book and placed it back on the stack. She left, closing the door quietly behind her. She felt as if she had been eavesdropping or spying.

Back in the guest room, she unpacked and made up the bed. She straightened the bathroom, although it was really not dirty. Wandering downstairs, she hesitated to disturb the silence by turning on the television. Finally, she set up the pool table and practiced for a while. She had just finished game two, when she heard Katherine's car pulling into the drive. She hurried to put everything away as if she were a child caught playing with something forbidden.

Elizabeth enjoyed the afternoon with Katherine. They talked about Alex as a child, Elizabeth's family, and the state of the world. The two women had a lot in common. Elizabeth was almost disappointed when she heard the car in the drive.

"They're home earlier than they planned," Katherine said, her eyebrows arching into little upside down Vs. Both were surprised at such an early return. Alex and Matthew McClintock were known for their timing. Either they arrived exactly when they said, or they were fifteen minutes late.

The kitchen door swung open, and Elizabeth stifled a gasp. Katherine's enthusiastic greeting covered Elizabeth's lapse as she jumped up and hugged her youngest son. Scott looked almost as surprised to see her sitting at the kitchen table as she had at seeing him come through the kitchen door. Her heart began to pound, so she took a deep breath to steady it.

"Scott! What a nice surprise!" Katherine pulled him over to the kitchen table and motioned toward the chair between Elizabeth and herself. "What brings you by?"

"I just thought I'd drop by to see my favorite person." Scott smiled at his mother and her smile widened.

"You old charmer you. You know just what to say."

"Well, it's the truth." The warmth of his smile filled the kitchen.

"That's sweet. You've met Elizabeth haven't you dear?" Scott turned to Elizabeth and nodded, but his smile had lost all its warmth. It seemed as though a bitter-cold wind blew through the kitchen. Elizabeth shivered.

"Are you cold, dear?" Katherine asked, concern shadowing her face.

"No, someone just stepped over my grave." Katherine's face wrinkled in confusion causing Elizabeth to laugh. "That's an old wives' tale which says if you shiver when you're not cold someone has just walked over the place where you will be buried. My mother used to say it all the time." The laughter fled from her face as memories washed over her at the mention of her mother.

"I'll have to remember that," Katherine said. She started asking Scott questions about his business and the house he was working on to ease the tension. Elizabeth swallowed her grief and looked up to find Scott watching her with—could it be?—compassion. Then the look faded and the cold hardness returned.

A sharp, howling wind whipped around the house, moaning like the voice of some lost soul. The voices in the kitchen stilled as they listened. Elizabeth shivered again.

"Your grave must be in a busy place," Scott noted. She

looked up in surprise. It was the first time he had spoken to her in a normal voice.

"You're probably right. With my luck, I bet it's under a freeway." For a moment, a smile flickered around his mouth then disappeared. It wasn't much, but Elizabeth's heart soared with joy. Maybe there was a chance. A chance of what? she chided herself. She was going to marry his brother. Well, at least they could be friends.

Elizabeth went about preparing dinner with a light heart. Scott had agreed to stay, and he was being friendly. Suddenly, the evening ahead took on a whole new glow of possibilities.

Dinner was almost ready at seven, but there was no sign of the two men. Katherine began to pace the floor. Matthew had said they would be home around six, but no later than seven. Matthew McClintock was never late without calling. Scott tried to push aside her fears, but she continuously went to the window to look down the long drive.

The phone rang, causing everyone to jump. They had lapsed into a silent vigil in the living room and the sound of the phone was ominous. Katherine hesitated for a moment and then hurried over to it.

"Hello. . .Oh Matthew, where are you?. . .Really!. . .That's terrible. . .Tomorrow morning?. . .Okay. We'll see you then. . . Good night, dear. . .I love you." Katherine hung up the phone and let out a deep sigh.

"What is it?" Elizabeth asked, still on edge.

"There was some kind of spill on the beltway. They were stuck in traffic for over two hours before the police allowed people to cross the median and return to D.C. Matthew said there were still a couple of things that needed checking so they decided to stay over until tomorrow afternoon and give traffic a chance to clear up."

"Oh."

"I'm sorry, dear. I should have asked if Alex wanted to speak to you."

"That's okay. He can call back if he needs to tell me anything." Elizabeth relaxed. Even though she was a little hurt that he hadn't wanted to speak to her, she was also relieved that he wasn't coming home tonight. She caught Scott looking at her intently. When their eyes met, he turned his head quickly.

"I guess that means more food for me," Scott said, slapping his hands together.

They returned to the kitchen and set the table. Somehow it seemed cozier and more comfortable to eat in there. Part of her was afraid that if they ate in the formal dining room Scott would return to his formal manner of previous weeks. They enjoyed a delicious meal of steak, baked potatoes, and salad. It was the best food Elizabeth had eaten in ages. Maybe it wasn't the food, but the company that made everything taste so good.

They soon had the kitchen cleaned up. Scott dried while Elizabeth washed and Katherine cleaned the table. Katherine finished quickly and went into the laundry room to put in a load of washing. They worked in companionable silence. Elizabeth daydreamed of doing this every night when she was married. The dream was short-lived when she remembered that Alex wouldn't be caught dead in the kitchen. They would have hired help to do all their cooking and cleaning. A frown appeared as she thought about it.

"Something wrong?" Scott asked.

"No. I was just thinking."

"It must not have been a pleasant thought."

"I was just thinking how nice it is to have a home." She knew it was true the minute the words left her mouth, but she hadn't meant to say anything. Somehow Scott brought her out of her self. She told him things that she had told few other people.

"I agree." He put away the last dish and threw the towel over the rack to dry. "How about a game of cards?"

Elizabeth was stunned, but quickly agreed. He told her that Katherine preferred to go to bed early, but would stay up to keep Elizabeth company. This way she could go to bed without feeling guilty. In a few minutes, Katherine came in already looking drowsy. When she saw Scott and Elizabeth playing, she made her excuses and went to her room. They played until after eleven amid laughter and conversation. It was just like before.

Since it was so late, Scott decided to stay over in his old room, saying he didn't want to leave them in the house alone. Elizabeth smiled as they said good night in the hall-way. Her smile was still in place as she drifted off to sleep.

৯

In her bedroom downstairs, Katherine McClintock's head was bowed in prayer. The minute she had met Elizabeth, she had known that Alex was not right for her. Over dinner she had realized that this was the Elizabeth that Scott had told her about several months ago. Putting it all together, Katherine had immediately known that this girl belonged to Scott. With that knowledge, she did the only thing a mother could do: pray. Her prayers lasted well into the night. At one o'clock she rose from her knees and got into bed with a deep peace in her heart.

twenty-two

Scott opened his eyes and blinked several times before he realized where he was: home. Gradually his mind cleared and he remembered the night before. Elizabeth. Last night he had seen again the lonely woman he had eaten Chinese food with in his house. Somehow he just couldn't keep himself distant. When she had mentioned her mother, the pain in her eyes made him want to wrap her in his arms and hold her. What was he doing? He hit the bed in frustration. She was going to marry Alex. The thought made his stomach twist like a pretzel. Maybe she had made a mistake by getting involved with Alex. He had probably charmed her into bed. She was so lonely that it wouldn't have been hard to be tempted.

He flipped over and buried his head under the pillow, trying to block out the thoughts. She was going to marry his brother. He had no right to interfere. He couldn't do that to his brother. Maybe Elizabeth was what Alex needed to straighten him out. Somehow he doubted it; the very thought made him want to hit something. He moaned. What was he going to do?

અ

Down the hall, Elizabeth woke up with a smile on her face. She hopped out of bed as the sun peeked over the horizon. She jumped in the shower, humming a tune. She didn't want to miss any of this day. Part of her wondered why she was so excited about this day in particular, but she ignored the thought and decided to just enjoy today. Tomorrow would come soon enough. She knew her next conversation with Alex would be a confrontation, but she didn't want to think about that today.

She dressed quickly in a pair of jeans and a navy pullover

sweater. She put on her favorite walking shoes and then straightened the room. Peeking into the hallway, she tiptoed to the stairs. Scott's door was still closed and there was no sign of life anywhere. Once in the kitchen, Elizabeth went to work. In no time, the kitchen was warm and full of the smell of homemade bread and brewing coffee. She set the kitchen table for three, placing each piece with a loving touch. She put out a glass pitcher of orange juice and one of milk, as well as the butter and jam.

Elizabeth paused to look out the kitchen window and her mouth opened in delight. The ground was covered in a couple of inches of snow. She opened the kitchen door, ignoring the cold, and breathed in the fresh air. There was a hush, broken only by the sound of an occasional bird. For the first time in a long time, Elizabeth felt a presence. She soaked in the feeling of being held in a cloak of love. She didn't even feel the biting cold, only warmth from an unseen arm around her shoulder. The sensation passed and she felt the cold air on her nose. Closing the door, she returned to breakfast.

As she worked, she could hear God's gentle voice. She knew this was what she wanted, what she needed, more than anything: a home. She needed a place that was all her own, not some mansion with a host of servants at her beck and call. There were going to have to be some changes in her relationship with Alex. The situation could not continue in the direction it was going. Alex wanted her to change to fit his life, but he needed to do some changing too.

With that thought in mind, she finished breakfast with the first peace she had had in months. She didn't like confrontation, but this was her life she was talking about, not some silly squabble over where to go on vacation.

She was just pulling the bread from the oven, when the door from the dining room swung open. Putting the bread on a hot pad, she turned with a smile. Her breath caught in her throat at the sight of Scott in the doorway.

"Good morning," was all she managed to get out.

"Good morning to you. You've been busy this morning."

Scott went to the oven and sniffed. "Something smells good."

Her heart thrilled at his words. "That would be the bread."

"Where's Mom?" Scott asked as he pulled a bread basket from the cabinet and proceeded to slice the bread.

"I don't know. I thought she'd be up by now." Elizabeth looked up at the clock. Half-past eight.

"She never sleeps this late. She gets up everyday at five-thirty." A worried frown creased his forehead in deep furrows. Elizabeth felt a sudden urge to smooth it away, but she caught herself before she moved her hand.

"I'll go check on her." Elizabeth went back through the living room to the master bedroom. Knocking softly on the door, Elizabeth called her name. There was no answer. She called her name a little louder and pushed the door open. Peeking around the door, she expected to see Katherine snuggled under the covers. Instead, there was no sign of her anywhere. The bed was rumpled, but no Katherine. Pushing the door open, Elizabeth walked into the room and gasped.

"Scott!" she yelled. She felt the world go black.

❧

Scott continued to slice bread while Elizabeth went to check on his mother. He felt uneasy, but he tried to shake it. The unease continued to grow, so he put the knife down and followed Elizabeth. He was just rounding the corner of the living room when he heard her scream. The sound was like a vise to his heart. He ran the last few feet, just in time to catch Elizabeth as she swooned.

His first concern was Elizabeth, so he didn't notice the crumpled form right away. He took Elizabeth by the shoulders and was about to help her to the bed when he saw his mother lying on the floor. He shook Elizabeth. She moaned and then sunk to the bed, her head in her hands, crying. Scott moved to his mother and checked her pulse.

"It's okay, Elizabeth. She's alive." Elizabeth sobbed, but regained enough of her senses to join him.

"Katherine. Katherine," Elizabeth called her name, but

there was no response.

"Elizabeth, call 911." She moved to the bedside phone and he checked for broken bones. He could find nothing to explain her condition. He called her name, but there was still no response. Taking her wrinkled hand in his, he began to stroke it and pray as he had never prayed before.

≈

It was several minutes before the ambulance made its way to the house. Elizabeth met them at the door and showed them to the bedroom. Within minutes, they were on their way to the hospital. Scott in the ambulance with his mother and Elizabeth following in the car. She had stopped long enough to turn off the coffeepot and the oven before jumping in the car. As she followed the ambulance, she was grateful that she had insisted on bringing her car.

At the hospital, they waited in the hallway for what seemed like hours, but was actually only minutes. Scott had grabbed her hand the moment she had entered the hospital and hadn't let go, as if it was his lifeline. Elizabeth prayed for Katherine to be all right. It just wasn't fair to lose two mothers so close together.

The doctor appeared a few moments later, his brow creased. Scott's grip tightened. As one they waited for the doctor to give his prognosis. He took his time, seeming to search for the right words. Elizabeth's unease grew with every passing second.

"Your mother has had a mild stroke. There doesn't seem to be any long-term damage. We'll want to keep her for a couple of days and run some tests to see what caused the stroke and to monitor her condition."

Scott visibly relaxed and then grasped the doctor's hand. "Thank you, doctor. When can we see her?"

"She's being moved to a private room, number 314. Why don't you wait for her there."

"Thank you." Elizabeth murmured her own thank you to God as well as the doctor. She squeezed Scott's hand and they walked to the elevators together.

It was several minutes before Katherine was wheeled into the room. As soon as she was settled, Scott leaned close and spoke to Katherine. She nodded, but didn't speak. She was still weak and groggy from the medication. Elizabeth stood beside him, her fingers intertwined with his.

❧

As Alex entered the kitchen door, a wave of foreboding struck him full force. The kitchen table was still set for breakfast even though it was almost ten o'clock. The milk pitcher was sitting out and the coffee was cold. His eyes scanned the room, taking in the details. The stillness of the house was eerie in its totality. Making a quick search of the house, he found everything in perfect order until he came to his parents' room. The normally neat room was in a state of chaos, the linens hanging off the bed and the dressing table looking as though someone had cleared the table with one smooth swipe. The shrill ring of the bedside phone jerked him out of his thoughts and he grabbed the phone.

"Hello?. . .Yes, this is Alex McClintock. . .What?. . .I'll be right there." He hung up the phone and then dialed Scott's number. No answer. He left a message on the machine and then strode through the house in search of his father. He paused in the kitchen to throw out the milk and clear the table before searching for his father in the garage.

His father's face paled as he related the news of Katherine's stroke. Then he pulled himself up and headed for the car. Alex persuaded him not to drive and took the wheel. Within moments they were speeding down the beltway.

The information desk gave them the room number and they rushed to the elevators. Alex reached the room first and quietly pushed the door open. The first thing he saw was Scott holding Elizabeth's hand. The two of them were leaning over the bed talking softly to Katherine. The worry for his mother was overshadowed by a sudden green anger.

His father entered seconds later and pushed past Alex to Katherine's side. Alex watched as he took her hand and whispered words of love. It was the picture of the perfect family. The adoring husband, the loving son and his faithful wife were all gathered around. Scott had usurped his place, going so far as to take his fiancée. Hate flickered across his features, but were smoothly replaced by a look of concern. He moved to his mother's bedside behind Elizabeth, circling her waist with his arm.

28

As Alex joined them, Elizabeth felt Scott release her hand. Her place was as Alex's comforter, not Scott's. She put her arm around Alex and squeezed. Scott moved away to let Alex closer. Elizabeth felt cold. The warm connection she had found with Scott was broken as he moved away from her. Alex's presence had pushed them apart.

It was decided that Matthew McClintock would stay with his wife; so that Scott could check on his house and Elizabeth and Alex could spend some time together and take care of the family home. Scott took his father's car, and Alex rode with Elizabeth. As the engine warmed up, she watched Scott pull away and disappear into traffic. Her heart went out to him. She couldn't say the same for the man beside her. She couldn't fathom what he was feeling right now. The moment he had entered the hospital room, she had realized that she really didn't know this man. He had never let her past a certain point. There was an invisible wall between her and the real Alex McClintock and it frightened her. She pulled out of the parking lot and into traffic in silence. The silence lasted the whole trip, for which she was grateful.

Back at the house, they ate a quick lunch and straightened the house. Alex, claiming fatigue, disappeared into his room. Elizabeth went to her room and paced the floor. Thoughts whirled around in her mind like a swarm of bees, never landing, always buzzing. On her third trip across the room, her eyes fell on a book on the bedside table. It was a Bible. She picked it up and sank onto the bed. With a prayer, she opened it up and began to read.

28

All the way home Scott prayed for his mother and gave thanks for her life, but another prayer lingered near his heart. With Elizabeth by his side, he had felt a comfort and peace. The peace and comfort of sharing his life with someone who understood. Then, in a moment, Alex's presence had shattered that peace. He was playing with fire. Elizabeth belonged to Alex and there was nothing he could do about it. He prayed for guidance and strength.

At his house, he checked on all the animals and set the house to rights. Then he grabbed his Bible and began to read. He read the words, but did not comprehend them. Finally, he closed the book and got on his knees. He poured out his heart to God for over an hour. When he thought he could do no more, he felt the hand of God touch him and peace settled on his heart. There were no answers to his dilemma, only the knowledge that he was not alone. He trudged up the stairs and fell into bed, exhausted.

❧

Alex spent the evening plotting. His mother's health never entered his thoughts. All he could think about was the image of Scott's and Elizabeth's hands intertwined. His lips were set in a thin line, and his eyes glowed like fire. He paced the room like a caged panther for an hour. Abruptly, he stopped and his face relaxed into a smile. He hadn't lost yet. As long as he kept in control, everything would turn out just as he had planned. He changed into casual clothes and smoothed his hair and expression. Then he went in search of Elizabeth. They had a quiet dinner in the kitchen and then watched television. He sensed the tension between them, but ignored it, maintaining his usual air of concern for her well being. He kissed her softly on the forehead before they retired and then got ready for bed. One fleeting thought of his mother passed through his mind as sleep claimed him.

twenty-three

Elizabeth awoke with a sense of peace. She had read several chapters in the Psalms and had been strengthened by them. As she read, she had realized that she had not picked up her Bible, except to go to church, since she had started dating Alex. Even then, she had hardly opened it because the preacher often spoke from one verse of Scripture which he quoted from memory. She only took her Bible out of habit. She had made a promise last night to begin every morning by reading the Bible. She remembered another such promise she had made and lifted a prayer for forgiveness.

Sitting up in bed, she reached for the well-worn Bible. The front cover fell open and she read the dedication: To Katherine, with love, Matthew. She caressed the cracked leather. Seeing a bookmark that she hadn't noticed the night before, she opened the Bible to it. It marked the third chapter of Lamentations. Verses 22-24 caught her attention. They said the compassions of God are new every morning and that our hope is in God. She felt a tug of remorse for her lack of faithfulness to God, after all he had done for her and his faithfulness to her. She prayed for forgiveness and guidance. She lifted her head, knowing that she had to settle things with Alex today. There would never be a good time, and if she didn't do it now, she was afraid things would never change.

She dressed slowly and cleaned the already clean room. Gathering her courage around her like a cloak, she moved to meet the enemy: her own fear. She found Alex in the kitchen with a cup of coffee and the morning paper.

"Good morning, sweetheart." He smiled over the top of his paper and then continued reading. She got a coffee mug from the cabinet and filled it just to have something to do with her hands. Taking in a deep breath, she joined him at the table.

"Alex, we need to talk." He lowered the paper, one eyebrow raised in a question mark.

"You seem so serious, darling. If it's about Mother, you needn't worry. The doctor said she will be fine in a couple of days." He patted her hand and then raised the newspaper again. It seemed to embody the heart of their problem, that invisible wall that separated them. She pulled the paper from his hands and folded it before placing it out of his reach.

"It's not about your mother. It's about us." She pulled herself up, her back rigid.

"Darling, if it's about going to your friends for New Year's, I think there should be no argument now. It's our place to be here with Mother, especially after what happened yesterday." The patronizing smile made her want to scream, instead she remained calm and thought out her next response.

"It's more than just New Years that I want to discuss. I think we should get a few things clear before we proceed any further in our relationship." The words sounded formal to her own ears.

"What exactly are you talking about?" His smile retracted into a frown.

"I think we should postpone the wedding until we can work through some areas of our relationship that I'm not comfortable with." She chose her words carefully. "I think we need more time to get to know each other better before we rush into marriage." There. She had said it. Alex said nothing and the silence made her uneasy. She had expected immediate opposition, anger, anything. Not this silence.

"I don't see the need for that. We know each other as well as we need to." He stretched across the table and retrieved the paper. "Now get that silly notion out of your head."

She stared in stunned outrage as he unfolded the paper and picked up where he left off. It took several moments for the shock to wear off. Then she stood up and ripped the paper from his hands and threw it in the garbage. Fire flashed in her eyes and was met by cool reserve. Their eyes held in a silent struggle of will.

"It is not a silly notion." Her voice had raised a hair, but she kept her temper in a choke hold. "I do not want to get married in January, but most of all I don't want to be talked to in that manner. I am not your slave, or your employee, or your dog. If we get married, I will be your partner and nothing less." The color began to flare in her cheeks and her jaw was clenched.

"What do you mean 'if,' darling? There is no if." His face was smooth and his hands were resting palms down on the table. Hers were clenched in fists.

"If there aren't some changes in our relationship, there will be no wedding."

"Don't be silly. Of course, there'll be a wedding. You're just under a lot of stress right now. We'll talk about it later, when you've calmed down."

"No, we won't. We're going to talk about it right now." The choke hold was slipping.

"All right, dear. What is it, exactly, that you want?" His patronizing tone loosened another finger. *Hold on. Don't let him get to you.*

"I want to be a partner in this relationship, not a junior partner. When there is a decision to be made that affects both of us, it should be made together. The wedding date for example. You didn't even check with me before you announced it in front of your parents. You didn't even ask me about going to your parents. You informed me like I was one of your shareholders."

"I don't see why you're getting so upset. I just wanted what was best for both of us."

"How do you know what's best for me?" She placed both hands on the table and leaned forward.

"Because I know you better than anybody else." His silky smile made her more determined than ever that the line would be drawn today.

"If you know me better than anyone else, why don't you know that I hate your house and all your servants? I want a home of my own, not a show palace. I want a place where my children can run and play without worrying about breaking a priceless piece of art." She paused for a breath, noting with satisfaction that his smooth facade was crumbling around the edges.

"What do you mean, you don't like my house?"

"I don't like your house, and I don't want to live there. I want some place that we can decorate together, someplace that is ours, not yours."

"That's out of the question. We will live in my house."

"You don't own me. I will do as I please."

"You're my wife and you will do what I say." There was a hard edge to his tone that she had never heard before.

"I am not your wife." He stood towering over her and then leaned down close to her face. They looked like two soldiers poised for battle, nose to nose in a standoff.

"In January you will become Mrs. Alex McClintock, and you will live in my house." She was suddenly aware of the kind of man she had been dating. For the first time she saw him for who he was, and she didn't like what she saw. Suddenly, she knew what she had to do.

"No, I won't." She calmly pulled the ring from her finger and placed it on the table between them. She turned to leave, but he grabbed her wrist in a viselike grip, wrenching her around to face him. She cried out in pain.

"I said, you will marry me in January and live in my house and that is final." His eyes burned with a hidden fire, and she felt fearful of him. The smooth facade was completely broken, exposing the real Alex McClintock. He twisted her arm until she cried out again.

"Let me go!" Her own temper overcame her fear, and she pulled back and hit him full force on the jaw with her fist. He released her to gingerly touch his jaw, and she ran through the house to her room, locking the door behind her. She held her breath, waiting for the sound of footsteps, but they never came. A few moments later, she heard the kitchen door slam. From her window, she saw Alex get in his car and peel out of the driveway. Her knees gave way and she sunk to the floor with her head against the wall. The tears came and she felt a burning shame rise up. How could she have been so blind?

She sat there for five minutes in numbed shock, tears rolling down her face. Then she realized she had to act. She dug through her bag and found the diamond earrings and necklace and placed them on the bed. Then she began to throw her clothes into the suitcase, stuffing them in without regard to wrinkles. She took her vanity case into the bathroom and threw all her belongings into it. She looked around to make sure that she had all her things and then peeped out the door. All was quiet. She quickly loaded her car and then made one more check of the house. Back at the car, she suddenly remembered the Christmas gifts in the trunk. She took out the gifts for his parents and put them on the living room table.

A sob of regret escaped her as she looked around at what had in the past few days become to feel like home. She swallowed the grief once again and headed for her car. She couldn't go home. It was too much to spend the holidays in the empty townhouse. She turned her car toward Hope's house. There was no other place to turn.

&

When Hope answered the door, she didn't ask any questions. She just held out her arms and pulled her into the house. That was all it took for the torrent of tears to be released. It was another half hour before she told Hope what had happened. Hope's face took on the expression of a mother bear protecting her young, but she didn't seem surprised.

"That jerk! You should be glad to be rid of him! I'm just glad you found out in time." Hope pulled her close in a hug.

"I'm sorry I barged in on you like this," she managed to choke out between hiccupy-sobs.

"There's no need to be sorry. I would have been hurt if you hadn't come here. Besides, it'll be great to have you for the entire holidays." She hugged her friend again and then blew her nose.

"I guess I should unload the trunk." Elizabeth sighed and a sudden weariness enveloped her.

"I won't hear of it. Jeff will get it. What you need is a soak in a hot bath, a nap and some lunch, in that order."

Elizabeth gave in without a struggle and was soon soaking in rose-scented waters. She relaxed in the water and felt the tension begin to ease. Despite the emotional war of the morning, she felt a peace descend. God had been trying to warn her for months, but she had ignored the gentle pleading of the Spirit. Her anxiety was an alarm, and now that she had obeyed, peace reigned. She almost fell asleep in the bathtub. She roused herself and got out of the bathtub, pulled on a flannel gown and fell into bed.

Several hours later, she awoke to a gentle tapping at the door. It was Hope with a bowl of hot soup and a sandwhich. As she ate, they talked about Christmas and made plans, but no mention of Alex was made. Elizabeth got dressed and then joined Hope in the kitchen. While they were cooking, Elizabeth covered her mouth when she remembered Katherine.

She explained to Hope about the day before. "I don't know what to do. I'd like to check on her, but I just can't face Alex right now."

"Let's call the hospital and see if they'll give us any information." Hope made the call, but all they would say was that she was stable. Not one to give up, she called the room directly. Scott answered and she told him that she was a friend of Katherine and wanted to get an update on her condition so that they could share the prayer request with their church. He told her that she would be going home the day after tomorrow. She thanked him and hung up.

Listening on the other phone, Elizabeth had almost gasped at the sound of Scott's voice. Her heartbeat so loud that she was afraid he would hear it over the phone line. As she hung up the phone, another realization came to her. It was Scott that she was truly attracted to with his warm and caring personality. He was the kind of man she wanted to marry. Not the *kind*, she reprimanded herself, the *man* she wanted to marry. The thought brought pain, because there was no way she could ever make that right. She had made a bad choice, and now she would have to pay for her mistake. How could she ever win Scott when she had just dumped his brother?

Elizabeth went through the motions of dinner and small talk, but her mind was elsewhere. Jeff asked no questions, for which she was grateful. Hope would tell him everything later. She excused herself after dinner and went to her room. She pulled out her Bible and read from Lamentations again. She felt a kinship with Jeremiah who had seen such unnecessary pain and destruction. If only the people had turned to God, none of it would have happened. It was the same with her. If she had listened to that first warning, then her life would be totally different. The word "if" was such a heartbreaking word. She curled up under the covers and tried to pray, but the words jumbled in her mind. Finally, one word passed her lips: help. Then sleep mercifully claimed her.

twenty-four

The rest of the holidays went by in a blur of cooking, parties, and gift-giving. Elizabeth tried to keep her mind off the entire McClintock clan, but as the end of the holiday's approached, her apprehension grew. How was she going to face everyone at the office? How was she going to face Alex? The more she thought about it, the more she realized that she couldn't stay at the firm. She would work until she could find another position, and then she would turn in her resignation. Once that was settled in her mind, Elizabeth could enjoy the holidays with her friends, but the gnawing unease continued.

New Year's Eve gave her a respite from her worries. All their old friends from college came over, and they played games and laughed and talked into the morning. Afterward she fell into bed exhausted, but sleep would not come. Tomorrow she would go home, and the next day she would go back to work. She tossed fitfully and finally managed to doze off as dawn was breaking over the horizon.

When she awoke, the sun was already high in the azure sky. She could hear a few brave birds chirping outside the window. Spring was still a long way away, but today was one day closer. There was something about New Year's Day that brought a sense of renewal, a time to start over. Last year she had made some bad choices, but today she would start anew. She reached for her Bible before she even threw back the covers, sitting up in bed to read. She read, "God is our refuge and strength." The thought comforted her, but she was still uncertain as to her next step. She flipped through the Bible aimlessly until it fell open in the Gospels. A phrase leapt from the page: "I am the way." She pondered the words. Jesus was her way. A peace stole over her heart as she realized that God would be her guide. She lifted up her eyes and prayed a prayer of thanksgiving.

She dressed quickly in jeans and an oversized sweatshirt and bounded down the stairs. She found Jeff with his eyes glued to the television, watching the pre-pre-game show.

"Well, good morning, sleepyhead," Jeff said. His smug expression reminded her of the Cheshire Cat from Alice in Wonderland.

"Good morning. What time is it?"

"It's late." He folded his arms over his slightly round middle.

"Funny." She cocked her head and folded her arms.

"It's ten-thirty. If you'd waited a little longer, we could have served you lunch in bed."

"Ha-ha. Very funny." She took a pillow from the couch and threw it at him. He caught it in midair.

"Maybe you should play for the other team." He grinned, and Elizabeth raised her fists as if ready to go a few rounds.

"Where's your much-better half?"

"She's in the kitchen." He had barely spoken when the commercials ended and Jeff was soon lost in game statistics and strategy. Elizabeth found Hope working on some game "snacks" for Jeff and his friends. They met every year to watch football. The array of hoagies, pizza, and chips 'n' dip suggested a feast, not a snack, as the boys were fond of calling it.

"This is more work than Thanksgiving," Hope commented from behind a stack of hoagies.

"Looks like it." Elizabeth moved into place beside Hope and they formed an assembly line for the sandwiches, making short work of them. Elizabeth took the leftovers and made her own Dagwood. At the smell of sliced ham, pickles, onions, and spicy mustard, her stomach growled in anticipation. Hope made one for herself, and they pulled stools up to the island and chowed down. They laughed at each other as the contents of the sandwiches threatened to burst out of the bread and mustard dripped from every corner.

"How ladylike!" Hope commented as a line of mustard made its way down Elizabeth's chin. She grabbed a napkin and wiped up the mess, choking back the laughter with her mouth full. She chewed and swallowed, while her hand waved like a fan in front of her face. Any moment she was going to break into hysterical laughter. "Don't do that when I'm eating," she gasped between fits of laughter, "or you'll be wearing my lunch."

"What's going on in here? I can barely hear the television," Jeff said from the doorway, crossing his arms and frowning in an effort to appear stern. "You ladies need to calm down."

Hope looked at Elizabeth. Elizabeth looked at Hope. Jeff realized what was going on, but was too late to avoid the barrage of mustard that flew from their spoons. It landed squarely on his nose and dripped down to his chin. He licked his upper lip and said, "Not bad." The girls could no longer contain themselves. They laughed so hard that tears flowed down their cheeks. It felt good to Elizabeth. It was a release of all the tension of the past months. By the time they had finished, her sides and her face ached from laughing.

They cleaned up the kitchen together and finished their lunch. Jeff set up the buffet on a card table in the living room. Elizabeth put off packing and loading the car for as long as she could, but she wanted to be gone before the guys showed up. With a hug and a promise to call, Elizabeth put the last load in the trunk and got in the car. Hope stood in the driveway and waved until she was out of sight.

The drive home was too short; all too soon, she was pulling into her parking place in front of the townhouse. She made three trips to the car, unloading all the Christmas presents and luggage. She smiled at the books from Hope and the bread maker from Brett. They knew her too well. Her two favorite things: reading and cooking. That was something Alex never knew about her. There were lots of things Alex didn't know about her. With a sigh, she pulled the painting she had bought him for Christmas out of the trunk and took it upstairs. She would take it back to the gallery tomorrow and get her money back or exchange it for something she liked better.

She dumped the last load in the foyer and made a tour of the apartment. Everything was just as she had left it. The dress from the engagement party still hung on the outside of the closet in its protective bag. She would return that dress. She would return everything. Taking the dress from its hook, she gathered all the expensive presents that Alex had lavished on her and piled them on the couch. She carefully boxed them up and put Alex's address on them. It would be simpler to take them to the office tomorrow, but the thought of handing them over in person made her feel ill. It seemed so cold, like a business deal gone wrong.

She spent the rest of the evening, airing out the apartment and unpacking. She ordered in Chinese food and watched an old movie on television. It had been a long time since she had been able to enjoy this simple pleasure. She curled up in her flannel nightshirt, robe, and slippers with a contented sigh. The thought of going to bed made her restless. Going to bed meant that tomorrow would come all the faster. She sighed and prayed for strength. Snuggling down in the darkness, she closed her eyes, but sleep was elusive. Every bad-case scenario she could think of wandered through her troubled mind. She finally fell asleep, but her tortured dreams kept her tossing all night.

The next morning she awoke with a headache and red eyes. It was not the best way to start this day of all days. She drug herself out of bed and got dressed. As she drove to work, her stomach began to tie into knots. They seemed to multiply as the miles passed. She pulled into her parking space and drew in a deep breath to calm her racing heart, but it had little effect. With back straight and eyes ahead, she marched across the remaining feet and into the building. As the door sucked shut behind her, she knew what the sound of prison doors must be like. Thankfully, she didn't meet Alex or his father in the hallways and gratefully slipped into her

office and released a long sigh. Her pardon was short, for she
had no sooner closed the door to her office before a light tap
sounded at the door.

"Yes," she called with as much confidence as she could.

Anne, Matthew McClintock's secretary, peered around the
door. "Mr. McClintock wants to see you right away in his
office." Anne looked uneasy and shifted from one foot to
another as she delivered her message and then scurried away
the minute Elizabeth nodded in response.

She knew that there would have to be some explanations,
but she was hoping that it wouldn't be this soon. Better to
get it over with now, she supposed. She stood up and
straightened imaginary creases in her suit, before making her
way upstairs. She took the stairs, hoping to avoid any
encounter with Alex. She entered the door marked "Matthew
McClintock, Senior Partner" and waited for Anne to buzz
the boss.

"Go right in." Anne motioned toward the door, her eyes
following Elizabeth into the office.

"You asked to see me?" Elizabeth asked from the doorway.

"Yes, come in." Matthew McClintock's face was frowning,
all the way from his eyebrows to his chin. Elizabeth tried to
swallow the lump of fear in her throat. She didn't want to
hurt this man who already had enough troubles to deal with,
but she knew he wanted an explanation. He sat silently for
what seemed an eternity, but was only a few seconds. "Due
to recent circumstances, I'm afraid that your services here at
McClintock & McClintock are terminated as of this morning.
If you are willing to keep personal family matters quiet, the
firm will issue a letter of recommendation to you. We would
prefer that you pack your desk and be gone before lunch.
Alex will be out of the office all morning so there will be no
unnecessary scenes. Do you understand?"

He spoke the words quickly so that she could not interrupt.
He obviously wanted no argument and no discussion. She
nodded. He didn't even look up as he said, "That will be all."

Her knees felt like jelly and there was a roaring in her ears, but she managed to look collected as she made her way back to her office. She looked around and realized that this was no longer "her" office. She choked back the burning tears that stood poised at the corners of her eyes and resolutely began to pack her desk.

She found a gift bag in the bottom of her desk and gathered her family pictures, cards from co-workers, and a sweater that she kept in the bottom drawer. All in all, it wasn't a whole lot to show for her time here. She put all the files back in the cabinets and arranged the desk in perfect order. Then she lay her office keys on top of the desk and turned her back.

Walking down the hall, she held back the anger and hurt that gnawed at her heart and throat. As she rounded a corner in a deserted part of the building, her eyes blurred and she ran into someone coming around the corner. A hand reached out to steady her and then quickly dropped. She looked up into the face of Scott McClintock. The coolness was back in his eyes as she knew it would be, but it still cut her already raw emotions.

"Leaving?" His cold tone and rigid posture gave added meaning to the simple word. She nodded, clutching the bag close to her like a shield. He started to walk on, but turned back. "How dare you? How dare you come into our family and do what you did? And with Mom in the hospital. I thought you genuinely liked her." She stared at him in confusion. Why was he so angry? Yes, she had broken up with Alex, but what did that have to do with his family? She hardly thought that Alex was brokenhearted. He didn't love her at all; he only wanted to control her. Now he was glad to be rid of her.

"I don't know what you're talking about." Elizabeth raised her chin an inch.

"You know exactly what I'm talking about." His jaw clenched and unclenched.

"No. I don't." She forced herself to look directly into his eyes.

"How could you pretend to be a Christian and then treat my brother this way. You came into our house and we welcomed you as part of the family and then you betrayed us like this." He paused and took in a deep breath before continuing. "Who was he? Somebody more exciting. Somebody richer or more powerful? What was it exactly that drew you?"

She gasped as she realized what was happening. Alex had lied. He told them she was having an affair with another man. No wonder Mr. McClintock had not even asked for an explanation. They all thought she was some kind of money-hungry hypocrite, playing on their good nature. Her gasp seemed only to incriminate her in Scott's eyes.

"Yes. I know. Alex told me everything. How he found you with another man while our mother was laying in a hospital bed. What kind of woman are you anyway?" His eyes blazed fire, and each word seemed to be a fiery dart piercing her heart. It was too much for her already taxed nerves. The tears burst forth like a broken dam and sobs chocked up in her throat. She couldn't even speak to defend herself. What was the use? He wouldn't believe her no matter what she said. She turned and fled down the hall and out the door. She ran all the way to the car and blindly pulled out of the parking lot. She didn't remember how she got home, but only knew a burning desire to get away from the condemnation in those eyes.

twenty-five

Elizabeth rolled over and squinted at the clock. Nine o'clock! That couldn't be right. She rubbed her eyes and looked at the clock again. It was the right time all right. A glance toward the window confirmed it. She hadn't slept this late in ages, not even on a weekend. She threw back the covers and was on her feet before she realized that she wasn't late. Then she crawled back into bed and snuggled under the covers. Just for today she would enjoy the one benefit of being unemployed.

As she lay in bed, she began to wonder about the future. All the doubts from yesterday flooded her soul and a wave of hopelessness washed over her. But as the fears took hold, a voice whispered, *"lo, I am with you always, even unto the end of the world."* The words repeated over and over in her mind, and a peace began to push the fear away. She got out of bed and got down on her knees by the bed. As she lifted her prayers to heaven, the fears disappeared completely and tears of joy fell from her eyes. She marveled that she could feel such joy when her life was a complete wreck. She picked up her Bible and read from the Psalms. Chapter after chapter were filled with David's despair over something terrible happening in his life, followed by his joy that God would deliver him. She could feel God beginning to heal her with His love. She felt it all around her. God was here and she would never be alone.

❧

Across town, Alex awoke to a pounding head and an upset stomach. He spent the better part of an hour moaning in the bathroom, trying to stop the spinning in his head and the waves of nausea that threatened to be his undoing. When his head finally cleared, he stumbled back to the desk chair. He caught his reflection in the mirror and almost didn't recognize himself. Gone was the calm, cool lawyer in a spotless suit. He had been replaced by a pale duplicate with red eyes and dark circles underneath. His clothes were rumpled and reeked of alcohol. Looking around, he saw several empty liquor bottles scattered around his desk. He held his head in his hands, trying to ease the pain until the memories from the night before jerked him to attention. No, it couldn't be true. He must have dreamed it. Panic seized him. For the first time in his life, Alex McClintock was afraid. Thinking back over the evening, he tried to think if there was any incriminating evidence. No one had seen him get in the elevator and he didn't remember seeing anyone in the hall. It would be her word against his.

Steeled by this thought, he started cleaning up the empty bottles and the desk. Then he took off his tie, shirt, and jacket. Going back into the bathroom, he splashed cold water on his face. He had just unlocked the door and entered the hallway, when the doorbell broke the morning stillness and sent a streak of pain up the side of his head. He stood at the foot of the stairs, holding his head, while one of the maids opened the door.

"I'm Detective Haney and this is Officer Dobbs. May we speak with Alex McClintock?"

"What can I do for you, officers?" Alex used his remaining strength to put on the airs he used in the courtroom. He could feel the officers raking him over and sizing him up with their eyes. They knew he had been drinking.

"We need you to come with us downtown. We have a warrant for your arrest."

"On what charges?" Alex tried to sound shocked, but his veneer of control was breaking up.

"Attempted rape." The words sounded like a death knell to his composure.

"You must be joking. I was here in my office all night." A plan was forming in his mind. "My fiancée broke up with me, and my mother has been in the hospital with a stroke." He managed a sheepish grin. "I'm afraid I've been drowning my sorrows." The detective watched him, but only shook his head.

"I'm afraid we have at least two witnesses who saw you at the scene of the crime. You're going to have to come with us." The other officer moved forward and began to read him his Miranda Rights. Then they escorted him to a waiting police car. He saw with dismay that all the neighbors were watching from their windows, and he slouched in defeat.

❧

Detective Haney looked back at the slouched form in the backseat. He had met Alex McClintock before, and the man sitting behind him looked nothing like him. Gone was the arrogance and high-handed ways. Somehow, it didn't give him the satisfaction he thought it would.

McClintock was still slumped in the seat when they arrived at the station. When they pulled him from the police car and led him inside, he followed like a beaten dog. Haney left him with Dobbs and went back to his office. A pile of paperwork and unsolved cases cluttered the desk, and the trashcan overflowed with wads of paper. He pulled out the case file from underneath the stack of reports that had mysteriously appeared overnight. He swore they were breeding. As he looked at the pictures of Carly, the finger marks on her neck brought a fresh surge of anger.

He remembered the way she had looked last night. Her eyes were the size of coasters, and her lip had trembled, but she had tried to pretend that she wasn't afraid. *How could anyone do that to another human being, much less a pretty young thing like that?* He looked at the picture one final time before closing the file. He needed to remember the victim when he dealt with the perpetrator. Yet, the image of McClintock being led away brought unwanted sympathy for the pathetic ghost of a man. He hit the desk with his fist. The resounding boom caused heads to turn, and he glared at the room before returning to the stacks of cases and the hum of the station returned to its normal, raucous level. Sometimes this job just got to him.

News of Alex's arrest reached Scott about ten o'clock. He was just about to leave for the southern border of his farm to repair some fencing when the phone rang. After a muted exclamation of disbelief and a few grunted questions, he was headed for the city. What in the world was going on? Alex arrested for attempted rape? He couldn't believe it! It must be a mistake. He knew his brother had faults, but he would never do something like this. Scott's face was taut, and his hands gripped the steering wheel until his knuckles turned white. He forced himself to loosen his grip.

Luckily, Alex had had enough sense to call one of his fellow lawyers, instead of Dad. Their parents didn't need any more stress right now. He would go down and take care of everything. It was obviously a mistake. He would clear it up, and then they would laugh about it when they told Mom and Dad later.

Scott entered the station with determination, but it wavered as he looked around. The waiting area was filled to capacity and the sounds of telephones, crying, and shouting stunned him into inaction. There were dirty faces filled with hopelessness and faces that looked no different than his own filled with confusion. For a moment he wanted to run out of the station. The pain and confusion that surrounded him burdened his heart until he thought it would explode from the pressure. This must have been how Jesus felt when he saw the multitudes. He took a deep breath and lifted a short prayer for help. Then he made his way to the officer in charge.

Scott had been waiting for almost an hour before his name was called. In the interim, his heart had been touched by the suffering around him. He forced his mind to focus on his brother as he followed the officer to the holding cell. When he saw Alex, he almost didn't recognize him. His face was drawn, with dark circles under his eyes. He had obviously been drinking the night before, and his suit looked slept in. The most disconcerting thing was the way his whole body seemed to slouch. He looked just like the people in the waiting room, and Scott's heart went out to Alex.

"Hey, big brother."

Alex raised his eyes and then lowered them again, remaining silent. Scott waited, trying to think of something to say. "We'll get this mess straightened out in a jiffy. You just hang in there. This is some kind of a mistake."

"No mistake, Golden Boy." Alex's voice sounded hollow and far away.

"What are you talking about?"

"I said it's no mistake. I did it." Alex looked up at him. "You look shocked, little brother."

Scott could only stand there and stare. Finally, he swallowed and forced words past his suddenly stiff tongue. "I don't understand, Alex."

"No truer words were ever spoken." Alex's disdain for his brother rose to the surface. "You never understood me. Mom and Dad never understood me. Besides, how would Golden Boy understand a mistake? You've never made a mistake in your life. You're perfect. At least that's what Mom and Dad always thought." He spoke as if he were talking to himself. Scott started to speak, but Alex interrupted, "You were their golden boy. Nothing I ever did was good enough. I was the eldest, but they wanted you to be the role model—you even took that away from me. I went to law school and graduated with honors. I joined the family business. That still wasn't good enough. You went off and did your own thing, but they always loved you more. This little incident will just prove to them that I am a disgrace."

"That's not true, Alex, and you know it. Mom and Dad love both of us."

Alex sneered and grunted in disgust. "Of course that's what you think. Golden Boy would never think his parents capable of fault. I bet you even came here thinking it was just some big mistake that you could fix. Well, you're wrong. You can't fix anything." Alex's voice rose with each word, until he was almost screaming.

The accuracy of Alex's accusation hit him full force, and he gripped the bars to steady himself. He struggled to think of something to say to convince Alex that he was wrong, but Alex suddenly changed tracks.

"Oh, Mr. Self-righteous would never think of blaming our parents, but he's sure good at judging other people." Scott's head jerked around.

"What are you talking about?"

"Elizabeth. It didn't take you long to drop her like a stone. All I had to do was hint that she wasn't all she appeared to be, and you turned your back on her. You look down your nose at everyone who doesn't live up to your standards."

Scott moved to stand in front of Alex, his hands gripping the bars between them. "What are you trying to say?"

"For a man with all the answers, you sure ask a lot of questions." Alex crossed to stand toe to toe with Scott, his eyes burning a hole in Scott's heart. His mind refused to listen to his brother, but his heart knew the truth. "I'm saying that Elizabeth and I were never intimate. Every time I tried, she pushed me away. She only agreed to marry me, because she thought you wouldn't have her."

"Why would you do that? Why would you marry her, knowing that she had feelings for me?" Scott spit out the words.

"That was the added attraction—for once I could take something from you. Not to mention the satisfaction of meeting the challenge. With a little grooming, she would have made a nice little wife. Someone to take to the social events and to entertain clients and do whatever I said. Unfortunately, she proved to be a little headstrong."

Scott held back the anger that welled up inside. If it weren't for the bars between them, he would have gladly choked his brother. "What about the breakup?"

"That was her idea. She seemed to think that she could choose what she wanted to do. I told her my wife would do as I said, and she said she wasn't my wife yet and never would be. I told her she didn't have a choice in the matter, and she threw the ring at me and left, just like that." His anger toward Elizabeth was evident in his eyes.

"The nerve of her," Scott replied between gritted teeth.

"Yes, the nerve of her." Alex's face was a study in calm. This was the face he had known all his life, a mask. The real Alex was the angry, desperate man he had seen a few moments ago. Elizabeth must have seen through the charming facade. "The two of you deserve each other." Their eyes locked for a moment, and then Scott turned away.

"I'll arrange for bail."

"Don't bother. I'm beginning to like my new quarters."

Scott turned sharply and strode down the hall. But halfway, he turned and retraced his steps. As he turned the corner, he saw Alex weeping into his hands, his shoulders heaving with sobs. Scott swallowed hard and slipped quietly down the hall.

Within moments he had signed the papers, leaving Tom Peterson, Alex's lawyer, in charge. Alex didn't want Scott involved, that he was sure of. He left the station with mixed feelings. Alex was obviously in big trouble, both spiritually and legally. His actions had been cruel and calculating, intended to hurt everyone around him, and yet, Scott saw the hurt and anger that had brought about his actions. Deep inside, Alex was a little boy who felt unloved and unaccepted by his own family. Scott knew he shared in the blame.

Elizabeth was another matter. His brother had been right when he accused him of self-righteousness. He had judged her and deemed her unacceptable. He sat in his truck musing over Alex's words. As the full weight of what had happened settled, Scott began to weep for his brother's sins as well as his own.

He arrived at home after two o'clock. His stomach growled, but he had no taste for food. He fixed a quick sandwich and ate it without tasting a bite. He went to his favorite place where he met with the Father. He got down on his knees and began to petition God. He begged for forgiveness. He interceded on behalf of his brother. But most of all, he prayed for guidance. The Spirit touched his heart, and he knew what he had to do.

twenty-six

Elizabeth was cleaning out her closet when the call came. She stared at the receiver in disbelief. *Alex in jail?* She hung up the phone and rushed to turn on her television set. The twelve o'clock broadcast was just coming on. The lead story was the arrest of attorney Alex McClintock for attempted rape. Elizabeth listened in shock to the details. She watched as Alex was being escorted from the station by his lawyer, Tom Peterson. When the clip was ended, she turned off the television and stared at the blank screen. A surge of relief flooded through her, followed by guilt. If God had not intervened and given her the courage to leave, she would have married that man. Her rejection could have sparked the anger that spurred him into action. But what could she do? She tried to pray, but the words and feelings were tangled into a knot. Finally, her soul became quiet and she felt an urge to visit the woman who was attacked. She tried to shake off the idea as a wild notion. But the idea persisted until Elizabeth grabbed her car keys and left the closet half done.

Halfway across town, she wondered what she was doing. Why should she visit her? How in the world could she help her? What could she say? She wasn't even sure where to find her. She had noted the address of the woman's apartment from a newsclip, but there was no way to be sure that she would be there. The Spirit urged her on. He had never failed her before.

Elizabeth took a deep breath as she entered the building. *Father,* she prayed, *how will I get in to see her?* Security was posted all over the building. She couldn't just walk up to her apartment, so she walked up to the security desk and asked for Carly.

"I'm sorry, miss. She's not accepting visitors at this time. If you'd like to leave a message, I'll take it to her."

Elizabeth hesitated and then answered, "My name is Elizabeth Jordan." She was about to leave her phone number when she felt a hand on her shoulder. Turning around, she saw a pretty blond with big blue eyes. A dark bruise marked her otherwise flawless skin.

"I'm Carly. What do you want?"

"I just felt like I needed to talk to you." The woman watched her for several moments and then motioned for her to follow. Once in her apartment, Carly seemed ill at ease.

"You're Alex's ex-fiancée, aren't you?"

"Yes, I am. How did you know that?" Elizabeth frowned in confusion. Carly sat on the edge of the couch, perched like a bird ready to fly at a moment's notice.

Carly told Elizabeth her story from the moment she met Alex at the airport until last night's episode. Her voice was steady, as though she were telling someone else's story. She finished by saying, "I just thought you should know."

Elizabeth sat dumbfounded. Her instincts had been right all along. To think he had been sleeping with another woman because she refused to have sex with him. Then when she had rejected him, he had taken his anger out on her as well. "I'm sorry, Carly. This was all my fault."

"No!" The word exploded from her. "No! It was his fault and mine. I knew about you, but I kept going out with him. I should never have slept with him in the first place. But mostly it's his fault. He needs help. I'm just glad you got out when you did." Carly's words faded as she finished, the moment of confidence fading as quickly as it had come.

"Nobody deserves what he did to you. It's his fault." Elizabeth reached out and touched the woman's arm. Carly looked up into her eyes, and Elizabeth could see pain and gratitude mixed with uncertainty. Something passed between them, sort of kinship, and then was gone. "What are you going to do now?"

"I don't know. They say I'll probably have to testify." Carly shuddered at the thought, and Elizabeth's heart went out to her.

"I want to do anything I can to help." Carly sent her a grateful smile.

"Thanks."

"Here's my number in case you need me." Elizabeth started to hand her a business card, but realizing she no longer worked at McClintock and McClintock she wrote down her number on a piece of paper instead. "Call me any time, even if you just need to talk."

"I don't know what to say," Carly said.

"Don't say anything." Elizabeth said good-bye and retraced her steps to the lobby. Now, she knew why the Spirit had led her here—he wanted her to know the truth. He had also shown her someone in need of a good friend. She headed for home lighter in spirit.

Elizabeth finished organizing the closet and cleaned two more before nightfall. She felt free at last from the worries and guilt that had plagued her since she had left Alex. He had made his choice and would have to live with the consequences. She had made her own. With her lifted spirits she had new energy which she put to good use, but now the energy was almost spent. One look in the hallway mirror told her she was in dire need of a bath. Her hair was falling out of a lopsided ponytail and a smudge of dirt was smeared across one cheek and most of her shirt. She felt hot and sweaty and ready for a nice hot, bubble bath. As she turned toward the bathroom, the doorbell rang. It was probably the Chinese food she had ordered. She grabbed her purse and ran for the door. Who cared what the delivery boy thought? She flung open the door and looked up into the eyes of Scott McClintock.

❧

Scott squirmed as he waited for her to answer the door. What if she slammed the door in his face. He couldn't think like that. He was still arguing with himself when the door flung open. He saw the shock register on her face and she just stood staring with her mouth wide open. He took in the smudge, the messed hair, and rumpled clothing and thought how beautiful she was even at her worst.

"May I come in?" He waited for her answer, but it took a moment for it to register on her brain.

"I guess so." She looked totally flustered. Her hand kept going to her hair or pulling at her wrinkled sweatshirt. Maybe having her at a disadvantage would give him the opportunity to say his peace. He followed her into the living room.

"So this is where you live? It's very nice." She made a noncommital reply and motioned toward the couch.

"Would you care to sit down?" The formality of the situation was beginning to get to him.

"Can't we just drop all the formalities and talk like friends."

"I didn't realize that we were still friends." The look of hurt on her face cut deep into his heart—he was the cause of that hurt. No matter how much he wanted to blame his brother, this was his own fault. He moaned and ran his fingers through his hair.

&a

Elizabeth had watched as he looked around and tried to make small talk, but his obvious distress tugged at her heart. She hated him for coming when she looked like this, putting her at a disadvantage. She smoothed the dirty sweatshirt and tried to smooth her hair, but it was no use. Her frustration came out in a sharp tone.

"I didn't mean to be so cross." Her admission seemed to lighten his mood. He looked at her and then crossed the room and put his hands on her shoulders. Gently, he pulled her down on the sofa next to him.

"I came here to apologize. It may be too late, but I need to ask for your forgiveness." She started to speak, but he motioned her to keep silent. She waited for him to continue. "I went to see Alex today. I guess you've heard about his arrest." Elizabeth nodded as he continued, "I didn't realize until today who my brother really is. He's a very angry and driven man who's managed to cover his true self with a mask of calm control. "

Scott stood up and walked around the room. As Elizabeth watched him her heart went out to him. Her love for him swelled to the bursting point. Hope, which had died months ago, sprang to life. Scott turned to speak again. "Alex told me what really happened."

Elizabeth's anger began to burn as she listened to the lies that Alex had told about her.

৵

Scott watched her face grow angrier by the moment. He prayed for help from above. She had every reason to be angry with him. "I know it's no excuse, but I'm sorry. I had no right to judge you." Scott waited for her reply.

"Of all the. . ." she sputtered, but her words died. He waited while she struggled for control. "How could he do that?" Scott stared uncomprehendingly. Then it dawned on him that she was angry at Alex and not him.

"Then, you're not angry at me? You forgive me?" Scott held his breath as he waited.

"Of course, I forgive you. You had every reason to believe your own brother. I, of all people, know how good he is at that." Elizabeth watched Scott's face relax in relief. Then a sudden doubt entered her mind—he probably felt convicted of judging her and only wanted forgiveness. Why would he want her as more than a friend? How could she even think of a relationship with him after what had happened with Alex? She struggled to hide her disappointment.

"You don't know how relieved I am to hear you say that." Scott smiled and her heart skipped. He hesitated and then asked, "Is there something wrong?"

"Nothing." She stretched her face into a smile. "I ordered Chinese food. Would you like to share?"

"I'd love to. When did you call?"

"About five minutes ago, why?"

"Well, that should give you plenty of time to. . .uh. . .

freshen up before dinner." He was trying to tactfully tell her she needed a bath. Ruefully, she looked down at her clothes. She had to agree with him. "Why don't you take a bath, and I'll watch for the food?"

She agreed and walked calmly to the bedroom, chin held high. Once inside, she flew like a mad woman, pulling out clean clothes. She rushed through her shower, all the while her heart beating out a hope. She tried to silence it, but it would not. Twenty minutes later she came out of the bedroom a different woman. When she entered the kitchen, she found the food spread out on the table with two plates and wooden chopsticks. The lights had been lowered and a short fat candle flickered erratically.

Scott led her to the table, seating her with a formal flourish. They ate in a somewhat strained silence until Scott accidentally dropped a piece of shrimp. It thudded to the floor. They both collapsed into relieved laughter, causing a piece of rice to stick in her throat. She made a choking sound and Scott was beside her in a moment. A fit of coughing sent the rice flying across the table. As soon as she was breathing right again, Elizabeth realized that Scott's arms were still around her. He kneeled down in front of her and held her hand. Looking down into his eyes, she saw something new in his eyes.

"Elizabeth, I have no right to ask, but I love you. I've loved you since I first met you. I know we've never talked about this—I don't even know if you love me too, but I just don't think I can make it through these next months without you by my side, and I don't mean as friends." Elizabeth tried to speak, but his words all came out in a rush. "I know that you are the woman God has for me in my life. I know the circumstances are not the best and any talk of a wedding will have to wait until things are settled down. But I've got to know if there's a chance at all for us."

Elizabeth's heart beat faster with every word. He had barely finished speaking when she threw her arms around his neck. "Yes, yes," she whispered into his ear. He pulled her closer, and she held on for dear life. "I love you too. I never imagined that you'd even look at me after I broke up with Alex. Yes, I want to be with you. Whatever comes, we'll be together."

"Whatever comes, God will be with us." Elizabeth smiled up at him. Yes, God would be with them. She felt a peace steal over her heart. She had made God her choice, and He had given her the desire of her heart.

epilogue

The courtroom was buzzing as Elizabeth pushed through the door. She moved toward the front and sat down behind the defendant's table. Katherine greeted her with a sad smile, patting her arm as she sank into the seat.

"You're looking good, Katherine."

"Thank you dear. I'm feeling much better. I was very lucky. God has given me a few more years yet."

"I'm so glad there was no long term damage. When I saw you on the floor that morning, I was so sure you were dead. You can't imagine how relieved I was when I heard that you were expected to make a full recovery."

"Well, I still have a ways to go before I'm a hundred percent, but. . ." Her voice trailed away as Alex entered the courtroom. She reached a trembling hand to the railing, anticipating his arrival. Instead, Alex turned and went in a conference room with his lawyer. She relaxed her grip and leaned back in the chair.

Elizabeth tried to think of something to distract her attention. "Where's Mr. McClintock?"

"He said he had some business to take care of, but he didn't say what business. He was behaving rather strangely this morning." Katherine's face wrinkled in concern. "Where's Scott? I though he was coming with you."

"He called and said he would meet me here. Come to think of it, he was acting peculiarly this morning as well. What are those two up to?" Elizabeth muttered.

"There's no telling with those two." A faint smile lifted the corners of her mouth, a slight drawing evident in the uneven smile. "You know you're going to have to quit calling Matt, Mr. McClintock," she said, motioning at the diamond sparkling on Elizabeth's left hand.

Elizabeth flushed and covered the ring with her right hand. Katherine reached out and took both of Elizabeth's hands, turning the diamond to the light. "You have nothing to be ashamed of, Elizabeth."

"It just doesn't seem right to be so happy at a time like this."

"Nonsense! I don't know anyone who deserves happiness more than you. After the way you've been treated by this family, I'm surprised that you have anything to do with us, much less support Alex."

"You have never been anything but kind to me, Katherine. As for Alex, I feel sorry for him. All those years of hiding his true feeling behind that cool facade must have been miserable. I'm just sorry that it had to come to this," Elizabeth said as she motioned to the bench.

"Well, I knew from the moment I met you that you were destined to be a part of this family. It didn't take me long to realize that you were with the wrong son."

"It took me a while to straighten it out in my own mind, but my heart knew it all along." Elizabeth shook her head. "I just wish I had figured it out sooner. Then, maybe this would never have happened."

"No, my dear. Alex made his own decisions. He kept that bitterness bottled up for so long that an explosion was bound to happen."

Just as Katherine finished, Alex and his attorney reappeared and made their way to the table. Alex glanced their way, but was unwilling to make eye contact. Elizabeth was so engrossed in thought that she jumped as a hand touched her shoulder.

"Didn't mean to scare you," Scott whispered

"You just startled me." She grabbed his hand as he settled beside her. Matthew McClintock slipped into the seat next to Katherine just as the judge was entering the court. "Where were you?" Elizabeth whispered.

Scott put a finger to his lip, motioning toward the bailiff. Everyone rose at the court official's command and then settled down to a hushed silence. "Alex McClintock, please rise," the judge commanded. Alex stood up and waited to hear his fate, his hands clenched into fists. After a long silence, the judge continued. "After a discussion with the D.A. and the victim, it has been decided that all charges will be dropped on the stipulation that you will submit to counseling and will refrain from practicing law for one year. It is the opinion of this court that sentencing you to a prison term would only cause more damage. The victim agreed to this sentencing with the stipulation that the defendant refrain from contacting the victim during this time. Do you understand?"

"Yes, your Honor."

"Good. Meet me in my chambers in twenty minutes to discuss the counseling agreement. Case dismissed." The sound from the gavel echoed for several minutes before anyone moved. Alex sank into his chair, his head resting on the table. It took only a moment before the McClintocks were beside their son. Elizabeth watched from her place as Mr. McClintock pulled his son up out of the chair and into a bear hug. Alex's limp arms soon tightened around his father. She could see tears flowing down his cheeks. The walls he had built around himself had fallen and left Alex vulnerable and unsure. Matthew reached out and pulled Katherine into the hug.

When they finally released him, Alex turned to Scott. "Well, golden boy, what do we do now?"

"I'm not really sure. I guess we'll take it one day at a time."

"Sounds good to me." Alex held out his hand and said, "truce?"

Scott hesitated and then took the proffered hand and pulled Alex into a hug. "Truce big brother."

"Does that mean I'm invited to the wedding?" Alex asked, his voice wavering.

"I think that's something you should ask Elizabeth."

Alex turned slowly, his eyes unwilling to meet hers. "Well, Elizabeth?"

"Of course you can come. You're family, aren't you?"

Alex's head jerked up and a weak smile trembled on his lips.

"I hope so. I really hope so."

"Enough of this mushy stuff. Let's go celebrate," Matt McClintock bellowed. As they gathered up their things, Elizabeth whispered in Scott's ear, "I have a family again."

Scott pulled her into an embrace and kissed the tears that had slipped from her eyes. "That's right and don't you ever forget it."

A Letter To Our Readers

Dear Reader:

In order that we might better contribute to your reading enjoyment, we would appreciate your taking a few minutes to respond to the following questions. When completed, please return to the following:

Rebecca Germany, Managing Editor
Heartsong Presents
PO Box 719
Uhrichsville, Ohio 44683

1. Did you enjoy reading *Elizabeth's Choice?*
   - ❏ Very much. I would like to see more books by this author!
   - ❏ Moderately
     I would have enjoyed it more if _____

   _____

2. Are you a member of **Heartsong Presents**? ❏ Yes ❏ No
   If no, where did you purchase this book? _____

   _____

3. What influenced your decision to purchase this book? (Check those that apply.)

❏ Cover	❏ Back cover copy
❏ Title	❏ Friends
❏ Publicity	❏ Other_____

4. How would you rate, on a scale from 1 (poor) to 5 (superior), the cover design? _____

5. On a scale from 1 (poor) to 10 (superior), please rate the following elements.

    ___Heroine   ___Plot

    ___Hero   ___Inspirational theme

    ___Setting   ___Secondary characters

6. What settings would you like to see covered in **Heartsong Presents** books?_____

_____

_____

7. What are some inspirational themes you would like to see treated in future books?_____

_____

_____

8. Would you be interested in reading other **Heartsong Presents** titles? ❏ Yes   ❏ No

9. Please check your age range:
    ❏ Under 18   ❏ 18-24   ❏ 25-34
    ❏ 35-45   ❏ 46-55   ❏ Over 55

10. How many hours per week do you read? _____

Name _____

Occupation_____

Address_____

City_____ State_____ Zip_____

Colleen L. Reece takes girls ages 9 to 15 on nail-biting adventures in the Nancy Drew style, but with a clear Christian message. Super sleuth Juli Scott and her savvy friends find love and excitement and learn that it always pays to have a sense of humor. The first two titles in this mystery series are not to be missed.

___*Mysterious Monday*—Julie refuses to believe her father was killed in the line of duty as a policeman. With the help of her new friend Shannon, Julie sets out to reopen the case.

___*Trouble on Tuesday*—Shannon has gotten caught up in fortune telling and an uncanny prediction. In spite of everything her friends try to do, only God can save her from this web of deception.

___*Wednesday Witness*—Being in the wrong place at the wrong time endangers Juli and her friends when they witness a bank robbery.

___*Thursday Trials*—Julie and her friends are called upon to be courtroom witnesses in order to keep the bank robbers from striking again.

········· Presents ·········

Great Inspirational Romance at a Great Price!

Heartsong Presents books are inspirational romances in contemporary and historical settings, designed to give you an enjoyable, spirit-lifting reading experience. You can choose wonderfully written titles from some of today's best authors like Veda Boyd Jones, Yvonne Lehman, Tracie Peterson, Nancy N. Rue, and many others.

*When ordering quantities less than twelve, above titles are $2.95 each.
Not all titles may be available at time of order.*

Hearts♥ng Presents
Love Stories Are Rated G!

That's for godly, gratifying, and of course, great! If you love a thrilling love story, but don't appreciate the sordidness of some popular paperback romances, **Heartsong Presents** is for you. In fact, **Heartsong Presents** is the *only inspirational romance book club*, the only one featuring love stories where Christian faith is the primary ingredient in a marriage relationship.

Sign up today to receive your first set of four, never before published Christian romances. Send no money now; you will receive a bill with the first shipment. You may cancel at any time without obligation, and if you aren't completely satisfied with any selection, you may return the books for an immediate refund!

Imagine. . .four new romances every four weeks—two historical, two contemporary—with men and women like you who long to meet the one God has chosen as the love of their lives. . .all for the low price of $9.97 postpaid.

To join, simply complete the coupon below and mail to the address provided. **Heartsong Presents** romances are rated G for another reason: They'll arrive *Godspeed!*